Livewire

Martina Murphy

PRAISE FOR *LIVEWIRE*

" . . . A classic and familiar account of
teenage-parent conflict and rock music."
The Kildare Times

" . . . Marks a splendid début for Martina
Murphy and certainly heralds a promising
writing career . . . "
Western People

POOLBEG

Published 1997 by
Poolbeg Press Ltd,
123 Baldoyle Industrial Estate,
Dublin 13, Ireland

Reprinted November 1997

© Martina Murphy 1997

The moral right of the author has been asserted.

The publisher gratefully acknowledges the support of The Arts Council.

A catalogue record for this book is available from the British Library.

ISBN 1 85371 757 6

Cover illustration by Leonard O'Grady
Cover design by Poolbeg Group Services Ltd
Set by Poolbeg Group Services Ltd in Times 11/13
Printed and bound in Great Britain by
Cox & Wyman Ltd, Reading, Berkshire.

For Colm, my best friend
and Conor, my lucky charm

Thanks to:

My parents and family, especially my mother who thought this was a brilliant book before she'd even read it.

Claire, word deleter supremo, and Aoife, my guinea pig reader.

All my friends – especially Betty for her great PR work at a certain wedding.

Frances Fox, a brilliant teacher, who gave me a love of literature.

Hayley, for giving *Livewire* its first book review.

Gabrielle Doyle, librarian at St Luke's.

And finally, all at Poolbeg, especially Nicole Jussek, for making my dream come true.

Chapter One

"WHAT THE HELL IS THIS?"

A flimsy white piece of paper was dangled before his eyes.

"Well?" his father demanded, eyes bulging, face red – in fact, getting redder by the second, Joey thought.

"They're me Mock Leaving Cert results, Da."

"CHRIST, JOE," his father thundered, making him jump. "I KNOW WHAT THEY ARE – I JUST WANT TO KNOW ARE THEY FOR REAL?"

Mr Boland glared at his son and then surveyed the offending piece of paper. "It says here that you've failed everything – Es, Fs, NGs, the lot – now surely that can't be right?" His voice was dangerously low.

Joey bit his lip, his green eyes glared insolently at his father. "It's right all right," was all he could say.

Mr Boland's fists clenched involuntarily at the tone in his son's voice. He sat down on the chair nearest him so that he wouldn't be tempted to do something that he might regret.

"How the hell could you have failed them all?" he asked in wonder and shocked disbelief. "What have you been doing all year – just tell me that!"

Joey thought it prudent to say nothing.

"Straight As in the Inter," his Dad went on almost to himself, staring once again at the report card that Joey had brought home.

"It's that bloody band!" he suddenly shouted, making Joey wince. "It's taking up too much of your time."

"No it isn't," Joey said somewhat scornfully. "It –"

"YES IT IS," Mr Boland was shouting again. "It's all you ever talk about – when you do talk that is – always playing your guitar in your room . . . oh yes, that band is the cause of this." He jabbed his finger at the report.

Joey shook his head and, anger creeping into his voice said, "You know nothin' about the band, Da – nothin', so don't criticise what you know nothin' about."

"I can when this is the result of your efforts in school." The results were torn in half and half again. "What would your mother have said – huh?"

Joey bit his lip and said nothing.

"I'll tell you – will I?" Mr Boland yelled into his son's face. "She'd have *crucified* you."

Both father and son were stopped in their tracks by the sound of a key in the front door. It was opened and a cheery voice announced, "It's only me," as the door was slammed shut.

Chrystal Boland, older than Joey by two years, entered the kitchen. She had bags of shopping with her and as she dumped them on the floor said, "God, town is crazy, but I got some great stuff all the same."

At the lack of response from either her brother or her father, she eyed them warily. "You two been fighting again?" she asked.

"Here," her dad picked up the discarded quarters

2

of paper and arranged them back together. "Take a look at this."

Chrystal came around the table to look and then gasping in surprise she turned to Joey. "You've failed all your exams – oh Joey!"

"Oh Joe is right," Mr Boland said gruffly as he stood up. "I'm getting out of here before I kill him."

He stalked out of the room without giving Joey another look.

There was silence after he had left. Chrystal turned to put the kettle on and Joey picked up the mock results and threw them in the bin. It was then that Chrystal whirled on him.

"How on *earth* did you manage it?" she asked angrily. "It's almost impossible to fail *everything*!"

Joey shrugged, a smile playing about the corners of his mouth. "I always did say I wanted to do the impossible."

She would not be drawn. "You are impossible!" she cried, "You're always rising rows and now this."

Joey gazed at her, his eyebrows raised. "Aw, come on, Chris, it's only me mock an' anyhow it's not as if I'm goin' to college."

Hands on hips, Chrystal glared at him. "Oh yeah – and just what are you planning to do?"

"Be a musician," Joey said matter of factly as Chrystal laughed.

"Oh yeah, you'll make a fortune at that all right," she said sarcastically, "Dream on, baby bruv."

Joey hated when she called him that as Chrystal well knew.

"Dad wants you to go to college, he has his heart set on it – sure after your Inter great things were expected of you."

3

Joey sighed – always the same bloody battle. "Well dream on, big sis," he said as he walked by her out of the kitchen.

Up in his bedroom he could hear the tea being made by his sister. He couldn't face going and having tea with three baleful faces glaring at him. Grabbing his denim jacket, he went downstairs.

"Don't bother about me for tea," he yelled to Chris. "I'm goin' out," and without waiting for a reply he was gone.

It was beginning to drizzle slightly and it was cold, but what could you expect for a March evening? Joey sunk his hands into his jacket pockets and debated with himself where to go. He could go for a walk in Marley, the local park, but it was cold. He could get chips in Alonzi's, but he was stoney broke. He decided in the end to go to Mick's, maybe he could even scab his tea from Mick's mother.

"Am I glad to see you!" Mick almost dragged him in the door, not even thinking it strange that Joey should be calling on him at such an early hour in the evening.

"Glad someone is," Joey thought with a wry smile.

Mick led him upstairs saying, "I've news for you but you won't like it."

They entered Mick's bedroom which was a dizzy array of posters of bands and cars, either stuck on the wall or standing up against it.

Joey sat at a desk that Mick was supposed to study at. Mick sprawled himself across the bed.

"Well, come on, what's the story?"

"Karen only rang me up, she's leavin' the band, the oul cow."

4

Joey jumped up from the chair. "WHA'?"

"That's what she said – she didn't ring Trev up 'cause she knew he'd flip, so yours truly was told the glad tidings."

"Bitch!" Joey said vehemently and then, "What the hell are we going to do now for a lead singer, aw shit, we're really sunk now. I suppose you had to cancel the gig for Sunday night."

"Had to cancel them all. Sure a new singer would have to learn all the songs. It just isn't possible to do it in so short a time. So we're a gigless band."

"When did she ring?" Joey was in shock.

"'Bout four o'clock, I was goin' to ring you but there's no need now."

"Did you ring Trev and Domo?"

Mick nodded. "Yeah, Trev went ape, you know Trev. Domo just said 'Aw well we'd better look around for someone else'."

"Typical Domo reaction," Joey mumbled.

"Eh, Joe," Mick said somewhat cautiously. "I do kinda have someone in mind. I told Domo an' Trev and they said that if you agreed we could give her a try out."

"A HER!" Joey said in exasperation. "I've had it up to here with hers." He made a sort of mock salute as he said this.

"She's a great singer," Mick persisted, "In fact we should have dumped Karen ourselves and asked her long ago."

"Anyone I know?" Joey was beginning to get curious now.

Mick nodded. "Yeah, as a matter of fact."

"Who?"

Mick took a deep breath and flung a silent prayer

heavenward. "Ann Corrigan," he tried to say confidently. He failed miserably.

"Ann Corrigan," Joey laughed. "Yeah sure, come on, Mick, get serious."

"I *am* being serious Joe," Mick said firmly, making Joey say incrediously, "Aw, come on, Mick, we can't have her!"

"Why not?" Mick's voice was calm.

"You know why not. Janey, Mick, we can't have her!" Mick had to smile at the desperate note in his mate's voice. "Why not?" he asked again. "She's a much better singer than Karen ever was. She can sing anything, Joe, I've heard her."

"Yeah, well she doesn't look much like a singer. At least Karen looked good. Ann isn't what you'd call even attractive."

"She is the best," Mick insisted. Going towards Joey he said, "Just think, Joe, you can write anything an' she will be able to sing it for you. Karen had only a limited range of notes – you know that."

This appealed to Joey. It would be nice to write songs for someone who could really sing. But why oh why did it have to be Ann Corrigan? It wasn't that he didn't like her – hell, he hardly even knew the girl. She was in his English and History classes and as far as Joey could ascertain she was definitely not this side of normal. Trust Mick to pick her to sing for them! Still, if she was their only hope . . .

"Well?" Mick pressed.

"Oh, all right," Joey agreed grumpily. "But if she's no good we dump her, OK?"

"Charitably said," Mick mocked. "Such enthusiasm."

Joey ignored him, instead he asked, "So when you goin' to ask her?"

Again Mick said a silent prayer as he said, "Well, I was kinda hopin' that you'd agree to do the askin'."

"*Me?*" Joey stared at his best friend as if he had gone mad. "Huh, the way you were talking a minute ago I was under the impression that it was as good as settled. If you think that I am goin' to ask some girl I hardly know to be in a band that she has probably never heard of, you are crazy. NO WAY, MICK!"

"Aw Joe –"

"No!" Joey was firm. "No way. Let's just put up an ad and ask for people who are interested to come to rehearsal. We can try them out then."

"That's too much bother," Mick was angry now. "You know that, Joe. Do you not remember the trouble we had when we advertised the last time? Everybody turned up, most of them hadn't a note in their heads. It was awful."

Joey did remember and it had been a nightmare. "Why don't you just ask Ann?" he asked.

"'Cause I don't really know her," Mick said and before Joey could butt in he said, "An' I figured if you asked her she'd agree quicker than if I asked her."

"How do you make that out?" Joey said. "Sure I don't know her either."

Mick looked uncomfortable. "Well, you're the best lookin' of us all, Joe. Anythin' you'd say would go down much better than if I said anything even remotely genuine."

Joey laughed. "Flattery will get you nowhere, pal – she'd be some fool to fall for that rubbish – you'd have all the women's libbers up in arms if they could hear you."

"Look, Joe," Mick was getting impatient. "You

7

know what I mean. Whatever you say, first impressions do count an' even if we said the same words they would sound better comin' from you. Now are you goin' to ask her or not?"

"Oh, all right then, I will," Joey agreed. Then, smiling, he said "But you're not *that* repulsive, Micko."

Mick ignored the joke as he pressed his advantage home. "So when are you going to ask her?"

"Janey, you don't rest do you?" Joey replied and then after some consideration he said, "I'll ask her tomorrow after French grinds. She goes to those ones me Da booked me in for."

"Talkin' of your Da, how did he react when he saw yer results?" Mick, now that he had got what he wanted, was happy to change the subject.

Joey put his eyes to heaven and said, "Aw, he flipped. I think he got a bit of a shock."

"I'm not bleedin' surprised – Even I was shocked. I know you never study but usually you'd get a 'B' or so. You never have to work."

"Looks like I never will either on those results!" Joey joked and Mick laughed out loud.

The two of them were still laughing when Mick's mother put her head around the door. "Tea's ready," she announced and then looking at Joey she said, "I made you some too, if you want to stay."

"Great stuff." Joey rubbed his hands together and turning to Mick he said "Did I ever tell you what a great slave you have in that woman?"

Mrs McPhearson clouted him playfully as she said, "I'll have you slaving for me after tea, washing and drying – why else do you think I asked you?"

After tea Mick asked Joey if he would explain

some Maths to him. "I know you failed them an' all, but yer great at explainin' things."

Joey sighed inwardly – of all things he wanted to do on a Friday night, Maths was not one of them. Still, he picked up Mick's Maths book and was soon trying to get through to him the finer points of differentiation.

It was about eleven o'clock when he left and Mick said, "If Ann does agree to sing, will you tell her to meet us in The Coach House tomorrow night? Domo and Trev can meet her then and we can arrange rehearsal times an' all."

"Will do," Joey promised, not at all sure that Trev and Domo would share Mick's enthusiasm upon meeting poor oul Ann.

Chrystal and Dee, his eldest sister, were up when he got in. They were in the kitchen drinking tea.

"I believe congratulations are in order," Dee said sarcastically.

Joey nodded "Yep – Chris said that I achieved the impossible."

He ignored Dee's – "Grow up for God's sake" – as he poured himself some tea. "Where's Da?" he asked. "Is he in bed already?"

Chrystal shook her head "Naw, he's gone out. Probably to drown his sorrows."

Joey ha-ha'd this remark as he prepared to leave the kitchen.

"Oh, by the way," Dee said "That girl rang for you again, Laura whatever her name is – Joe, will you ever ring her back, she has us persecuted."

"She has me persecuted," Joey said over his shoulder as he thought to himself, "Janey, what a bleedin' awful end to an awful day."

Chapter Two

"Get up Joey – you've got to go to your French grinds."

Chrystal was better than any alarm clock. "Yeah, yeah," Joey mumbled, still in a daze.

As sleep gradually ebbed away he did in fact remember that he had to go to French grinds this morning. He had to ask Ann would she try for the band. "Great," he mumbled dejectedly as he pulled on his clothes.

He was downstairs at eight thirty. "You'd better get your skates on," Chrystal commented. "Or you'll be late."

"I haven't been late yet," Joey said by way of a reply. This was true only by virtue of the fact that Joey hadn't actually been to the grinds yet. For the past five Saturdays he had left the house at eight forty-five and wandered around aimlessly until ten o'clock. He had then returned with answers made up to the questions his da would ask him. "I can see how much your French has improved," his Dad had said to him. Joey had problems keeping a straight face.

He left the house at eight forty, French books tucked under his arm as he cursed Mick for forcing him to go to these bloody classes this morning! He was so busy berating Mick in his mind that he was oblivious to the glances that were thrown his way from admiring females.

Six foot tall with corn blond hair, he was indeed "a fine thing thing" as half the girls in sixth year had labelled him.

He arrived at the grinds just in the nick of time. It was just as boring as he had thought and he had trouble keeping his eyes open. He was saved from falling asleep by a nudge from an amused girl who was sitting beside him. He sighed with relief when it ended.

Once outside he tried to locate Ann. He saw her in the distance walking with one of her friends. He ran to catch up with her. Tipping her on the shoulder he said, "Hiya, Ann, do you mind if I ask you somethin'?"

When she turned around, Joey nearly died with shock. The girl was a space cadet. She looked like an advert for Persil Colour. Her jeans were purple as were her boots. She wore a vivid pink sweat shirt and mad pink lipstick. Her hair was sticking out in all directions.

Ann's eyes widened with surprise when she saw who it was. "What is it?" she asked, eyebrows raised.

Her friend was agog and Joey felt acutely embarrassed. He really didn't know Ann that well. "Eh, can I speak to you alone?" He looked pointedly at Ann's friend who said somewhat huffily, "Don't mind me, I was just going." She marched off, head in the air.

Ann wasn't too impressed with him banishing her friend in that manner, Joey could tell. Again he cursed Mick silently.

"Well what do you want?" Ann demanded in a

none too friendly manner as she looked at her watch. That was bright yellow.

Ten tonnes of charm wouldn't work on her, Joey thought rather uncharitably. However, he smiled at her as he said, "Well it's rather, eh, Ann, did you hear that I was in a band – well not just me, Mick McPhearson as well, you know, from school – well us an' two other guys?"

"Yeah, *Livewire* or something isn't it?"

Joey nodded. *"Livewire,* that's right."

There was a silence as Joey tried to find the right words to ask her. This was harder than he had thought it would be, she hadn't even given him so much as a smile yet.

"Well," Ann was staring at him, "So?"

Joey noticed her clear candid blue eyes then. There would be no bullshitting this girl. She was really unnerving him and she seemed to know and enjoy it.

"The thing is," he began, wishing the ground would open up and swallow him. "The thing is, our lead singer did a runner an' Mick reckons that, well, we all reckon, that it would be a good idea if you, well, if you would audition for us as our new singer." There, it was said, he could relax now.

Ann's eyes narrowed. "Is this some kinda joke, Joe Boland, cause if it is –"

Joey shook his head. "No, honest Ann. Why would I play a joke like that? We really do need a lead singer an' we reckon that you're our best choice."

Ann smirked. "But why me?" she asked innocently.

Joey felt as if his feet had been whipped from

under him. This girl's frankness was unnerving. "Well, we reckoned that we wouldn't need a lightin' rig if you wore some of that gear onstage." He pointed to her clothes.

Ann laughed then. "Just as well I don't insult easily," she grinned. Then folding her arms and sizing him up she said nochalantly, "I suppose I'll give it a try, but you had better be good, cause I'll not sing with a second rate band."

Joey couldn't believe that she had agreed. Mick would at least think that he had charmed her. What a relief! "We're great," he said. "You won't regret this, Ann."

Ann smiled at him, a genuine smile this time. She didn't look half bad when she smiled, Joey thought. "We'll be in The Coach House tonight at eight, if you can make it. You can meet the other lads then and we can discuss giving you a tryout, all right?"

"Fine, I'll be there," she promised.

He had trouble locating the others. Trev was the first to spot him. "Joe, over here."

Joey made his way towards them after first asking Cathy, a lounge girl, to get him a pint of lager. Mick was mad about Cathy but he could never pluck up the courage to ask her out. Joey thought it would give Micko a bit of a thrill to have her come over to their table.

Joey was low on funds that night. He'd had to borrow this fiver from Chris and it had to last him the whole night.

"How's it goin'?" he asked them all as he sat down.

"Is Ann comin'?" Mick asked him anxiously.

13

"'Course she is," Joey said confidently.

"Did she mind?"

"Naw," Joey shook his head. "The Boland charm 100% effective."

The other three groaned but Joey, spotting Ann, hushed them up, afraid that she would ask what the joke was. He had a feeling that she would not appreciate it.

Ann came over to them and smiled at Joey who patted the seat beside him saying, "Sit down an' I'll introduce you to everybody."

When she was sitting Joey began the introductions. "Well, you know Mick." Ann nodded as Mick grinned at her. "You don't mind us askin' you to try out, do you?"

She shook her head smiling. "No, I was kinda flattered actually."

"The guy with the ugly face and dirty blond hair is Domo," Joey continued. Domo smiled good naturedly as he stuck out his hand. "How you doin'?" he tried to say naturally, without gawking at the girl's colour scheme.

"An' the bossy boots of the band is Trev," Joey finished, indicating a tall dark attractive-looking guy about twenty-two or so.

"I wouldn't be so bossy if you an' Mick were on time for rehersals once in a while," Trev said as he too, took Ann's hand in his own and shook it vigorously. Once the greetings had been exchanged it was down to business. "Have you got that song that you said you'd written?" Trev asked.

"Yeah I have it somewhere all right," Joey stood up and dug his hands into his jeans pocket.

"That's what I like about him," Trev whispered in Ann's ear. "He's so organised."

14

Ann stifled a giggle as she watched Joey look through all his pockets and then start rifling through the ones in his denim shirt.

"Have it," he announced triumphantly, as he produced a crumpled piece of paper from his back pocket and then proceeded to smooth it out on the table.

"Here," he shoved it at Trev. "The music is on this other sheet." He produced more crumpled paper and handed it to Trev. Trev sighed and began to flatten the paper before declaring, "I still can't read your writing." So with Joey telling him the odd word here and there, they went through it. "It's good," he eventually pronounced as he grinned at Joey. He handed it to the others whilst explaining to Ann, "Joe writes all our stuff – he's great at it really – if you can read the writing!"

Ann laughed as she took the paper from Trev. The four lads looked at her eagerly as she was reading it. When she looked up her eyes were shining. "It's really good, I like the music," she sounded surprised, and then she asked, "Did you really write it?"

Joey grinned. "Yeah, why do you find that hard to believe?"

He was gratified to see her go slightly red, it kinda made up for how she had treated him today. He was knocked off balance by her answer.

"Frankly yeah, I am surprised, Joe. I never thought that you'd be able to write such good stuff." This was said with such charming sincerity that it was impossible for Joey to take offence from it. The other lads laughed as Joey said, "There are a few things I can do that might surprise you even more, Miss Corrigan."

15

This time she really blushed, as she said, "Well, I don't think I really want to know about those things, thank you!"

"OH SHIT," Joey startled them.

"Wha'?"

"What's wrong?"

"It's Laura flippin' Peters," Joey whispered desperately. "Aw no, she's seen me." His attempt to duck behind Mick did not work. Laura was on her way over.

There was a groan from all the males present. Though Trev and Domo had never seen Laura before, they had heard plenty about her from Joey. First, on an ego trip because this girl had kept ringing him, he had jokingly told the lads all about her. Then as the days merged into weeks, and weeks into months, and she had continued ringing, Joey had begun to loose his patience. He had called her none too flattering names and Domo and Trev had slagged him saying that the girl must have little or no taste or that she must be desperate. This was their chance to meet Laura in person.

They were stunned, as Laura did not look like a girl that would ever be desperate. Her clothes were expensive, her figure desirable and her face gorgeous. It was when she opened her mouth that the illusion shattered. She had a high-pitched excitable voice that gradually grew more irritating the longer you listened.

Joey was irritated before she even spoke.

"Hiya, Joe," she said in a breathy feathery voice.

"Hi," Joey spoke in a monotone.

"How are you?"

"Fine," he gulped trying to sound bored.

"How'd you do in the exams?" she was looking for a space to sit down. Joey could feel panic rising in him. He could see Mick trying not to laugh.

"Well?" Laura asked, "How'd you do?"

"Huh?"

"In the exams, silly," she giggled.

"Failed 'em all," Joey gazed at her steadily.

She gave a nervous giggle as Mick tried to stifle a laugh. He began to cough. Laura looked at him suspiciously and then a smile lighting up her face she said, "Come on – I know you're only joking," she pushed him playfully. "Now what did you really get?"

Domo gave a loud guffaw which he tried also to turn into a cough. Joey shot him a murderous look.

"I told you," he said firmly. "I failed them all – have you a problem with that? I can't help it if I'm stupid." He gazed at her steadily.

Laura went red, she turned to Mick. "How'd he do, really?"

"He just told you," Mick replied, unable to trust himself to say anymore.

Laura tried to smile brightly then. "Ah well, you'll probably do better in the Leaving."

"Shouldn't think so," Joey said and then he turned from her and began to talk to Mick. Surely the girl would get the hint and go!

Laura didn't know what to do. Her gaze swept around the table and her eyes widened in surprise when she saw Ann there. Her expression was one of deep distaste. "I never knew you hung round with *her*!" she said gawping at Joey. Then, sticking her nose in the air she flaunted off.

Trev gave a low whistle. "Wow, she is gorgeous, Joe! Why the hell don't you just go for it?"

"She is as irritating as hell, for one," Joey said as he took a gulp from his pint.

"Yeah, an' she's the love of Jim Kendell's life," Mick continued. "You don't want to cross him, Joe."

Joey laughed. "That guy is an asshole. He wouldn't bother me. Janey, I'd be more scared of Laura than I'd be of him."

The others laughed, even Ann who had been privately mortified for Laura. She knew Laura from school and she had never thought that the girl could have been so stupid. Imagine letting a fella know that you were mad after him. Ann couldn't understand it.

At ten o'clock Ann said that she had to leave. She told them that she would see them down at the School Hall the next day. They all said goodbye and she left.

"What do yez think?" Mick asked them anxiously.

Trev and Domo looked at each other and Trev eventually said, "She looks a bit weird – are you sure she can sing?"

Mick looked at them in exasperation. "'Course she can. Look lads, I know she's not great lookin', but I'm telling yez it won't matter. She really has a great voice."

"Yeah, well, we'll take your word for it," Trev said reluctantly.

"I think we kinda hoped for someone a bit more like Karen," Domo put in.

"Aw, here," Joey laughed. "Please, anything's better than Karen. We hadn't what you'd call a smooth working relationship."

"Understatement of the year," Mick agreed. "Ann will be easier to get along with. I can tell!"

Joey, thinking of her only that morning mumbled to himself, "I wouldn't bet on that."

Chapter Three

That Sunday Joey had to sneak out of the house to go to rehearsal. It was two forty-five. Mick was waiting at his gate. "Oh God Joe, are you ever on time for anything? Trev is gonna go mental."

"Had to wait till me Da was out of the way before I could go out," Joey replied. "He's comin' down on me really heavy these days – he discovered yesterday that I don't go to those French grinds – he was pretty mad this morning."

"Yeah?" Mick was curious.

"Yeah," Joey looked glum. "Of all the fellas he runs inta when he plays squash, the bleedin' French teacher happened to be one of them."

Mick laughed. "An'?" he pressed.

Joey spread his arms wide. "He says 'Aw, Mr Duprés, how's Joe doin' in the grinds?'"

Mick cracked up laughing. Joey was a great mimic.

"An' Mr D looks blank. He tells me Da that he saw me once an' that I had trouble stayin' awake. Then me oul fella comes home in a tearin' rage." Joey grinned at Mick's laughing face. "It was not pleasant Mick. I kid you not."

Mick broke into a trot. Then he said, "I'm surprised he even let you out."

"He hasn't," Joey said ruefully. "I was ordered to stay in all day an' study, but then he goes out this afternoon, to Uncle Dick's, I suppose, an' he said to Chris that he won't be back till late. Chris goes out with her latest fella and Dee goes out with Tom an' so, here I am." He grinned at his friend.

Mick merely said, "I just hope you don't get caught."

"Let me worry 'bout that." Joey was nonchalant.

They began to jog to the school where they rehearsed. The principal let them store their equipment in the study hall.

They arrived on time. Trev was late. They grinned at Ann, who was looking a bit nervous, and then Mick asked where Trev was.

"Dunno," Domo grinned. "He won't live this down."

Trev was excited when he arrived. He was waving an issue of *Hot Press* around and asking if any of them had seen it. They shook their heads.

"Well, look here!" He was rifling through the pages and then he came to the one he wanted. He shoved it at Joey, "Look!"

A grin lit up Joey's face as he read the article Trev had pointed out. It said: "Any bands out there interested in becoming famous? If so, then this is the competition for you!!! Just submit a demo tape, along with lyrics, and you could get the chance to be in the final of a lifetime!!!" Joey skimmed through the rest of the article and then looking up, his eyes shining. He asked, "Do you think we should enter it then?"

"Bleedin' right, I do," Trev was totally on a high. "Three grand for the winner an' a recordin' contract, we'd be mad not to enter!"

There was a silence and all eyes turned to Ann who was reading the article.

Joey gave a half grin. "I think we have a problem in that we've no bleedin' lead singer, as yet."

Ann put the magazine on the table and shrugging said, "I thought this was my audition – yez might have a singer in about ten minutes' time."

Trev laughed and handed out copies of Joey's song which his younger sister had written out in her neat handwriting.

He handed each of them a copy, saying to Joey as he did so, "Janice says your writing is getting harder to read by the week."

Joey shrugged and replied in a mock serious tone, "Did yez never hear it said that really brainy people have awful writin'?"

"Naw," Mick said. He looked questioningly at the others and they too shook their heads. "Tough luck Joe – no one believes you."

"Joe," Trev was once again back to business. "Play an intro for Ann, the first couple of lines or somethin'."

"Sure thing," Joey took his guitar from its case and plugged it into the speakers. He ran his fingers lovingly over its strings and a series of deep vibrant notes came out. He then looked directly at Ann asking, "You ready?"

Ann nodded. Her heart was thumping. "Oh God," she prayed, "don't let me make a mess of this."

Joey played two lines of the song and then nodded to her to start. When she began, he almost stopped playing with the shock of hearing her sing. WOW – Mick was right! That was some voice. The things he could write for her! Janey, she was great!

"Not bad," he said graciously as the song ended. "It was OK for a first try."

Ann half sneered at him. Joey got the feeling she wasn't too keen on him. "Thanks a lot," she replied.

Joey didn't know whether she was being sarcastic or not.

"I think you were great," Mick said enthusiastically as he looked at Trev and Domo.

They too nodded their agreement.

"Well, Ann," Trev asked, "what do you think? I know we all think that you're good. Would you like to sing for us or do you want time to think about it?"

Ann grinned. "No, I don't need time. I like the song and if the others are as good, I think I just might stay."

Joey glanced at Mick. He was beaming from ear to ear. Joey felt ashamed of himself for the things he'd said about Ann. The girl was a great singer. Mick had been right.

Trev was in his element. The girl was heaps better than Karen an' so what if she looked a bit unusual, weren't singers supposed to look different? Anyhow, once she sang, you wouldn't even notice. He looked at her questioningly. "You interested in this competition so?" he asked her.

"Sure I am," Ann said. "The prize is great – it's worth a try, even for the experience."

The four lads grinned delighedly at her. Trev bit his lip and began once again to discuss business.

"Joe, we need at least two other songs for the demo tape, which has to be in by the end of the month, do you think you can do it?"

Joe looked at Trev as if he had gone mad. "How do I know that? Look Trev, the way I write is that if a tune or a word or somethin' comes to me, I write, if not, well then I can't force myself."

"We need two songs, Joe," Trev insisted.

"I can't guarantee it," Joey retorted, slightly irritated. Trev annoyed him when he started this crack.

He just couldn't understand that it was impossible for him to write when his mind was a blank.

"I suppose we'll have to use the old songs that Karen use to sing then!" Trev sounded annoyed.

"There's nothin' wrong with those songs."

"I know, it's just that Karen's voice was so limited that, well, you can write better stuff for Ann."

Joey sighed. "I'll do me best – that's all I can say, Trev."

"Right," Trev conceded. Joe exasperated him, he always made a big deal about writing a few songs, but then again, they were always bloody good songs, an' he, Trev, couldn't write them, not if he sat down for a year.

"Do you want fast or slow songs or what on this demo tape?" Joey broke into his chain of thought.

"Whatever comes into your head, just write it!" Trev grinned at him as Joey laughed good naturedly.

"We might as well rehearse this song," Trev indicated the paper. "OK lads," he said. "Let's see if we can get the ball rolling – Domo, you start us off."

Domo began to do the opening drum beat. Mick was on synthesiser, Joey on lead guitar and Trev on bass guitar. It took a bit of time to arrange the instruments but eventually Trev and Joey agreed on how it should be done. To the untrained ear the first run through sounded near perfect, but Joey and Trev were highly critical of it. "No way," Trev yelled in the middle of the song. "It's too slow – Ann, speed up the singing an' Domo for cryin' out loud will you get some life into those drum beats." Domo made a face at him behind his back, but nevertheless his playing improved.

This went on for the next two-and-a-half hours until both Joe and Trev were satisfied.

They clapped each other at the end and they made arrangements to meet again on Wednesday at eight o'clock for the first bash at preparing a demo tape.

"It doesn't specify that it has to be done in a studio, which is just as well as I don't think we could afford it," Trev concluded. "We'll just try to do the best job we can here. After that, we play live, in front of judges an' then if we get as far as the final, we'll be on telly."

They began to pack their gear then, all chatting eagerly about the competition.

Joey and Ann ended up walking home together as Mick had to go to the shops for his mother. He bid them both goodbye and left. Joey packed up his guitar and looked at Ann. "Comin'?" he asked. She jumped down from the desk that she was sitting on and joined him at the door. Joey locked up and dropped the keys into the caretaker's house, which was just beside the school, and they started to climb the hill toward their housing estate.

Ann gazed at Joey; she had to admit that she liked him. She hadn't up to this. He got on her nerves in school. He was terribly popular, not just because of his looks – there was something else, some charm he possessed that drew people to him. Ann had never had much time for him, believing that he was a terrible poser and show-off. But since yesterday morning when she had been asked to join the band she had been forced to change her opinion of him. It was true that he was a joker and messer, but Ann saw that it was just in his nature. He had been funny in the pub last night but it was today that made her like him. He was so dedicated to the band and he was a brilliant guitar player.

"Penny for them," Joey butted in on her thoughts.

Ann could feel herself blushing. "Oh, nothing," she replied. There was a silence, neither of them knew what to say to the other. Eventually Ann ventured, "I love your guitar. It's fab. Did you buy it yourself?"

Joey shook his head. He ran his hand over the case and said in a quiet voice, "Naw. Me Ma bought it for my fifteenth birthday."

Ann could have kicked herself. Trust her to bring up the wrong subject! In with both feet as usual. Everyone knew that Joe Boland never talked about his mother. "It's lovely," she finished lamely.

Joey, to her surprise, smiled. "Thanks," and then he said, "You do sing well, you know. I'm glad you said you'd sing in our band. Did you get your voice trained?"

Ann was astonished. After Joey had said "Not bad" to her rendition of his song she had been convinced that he wasn't too impressed with her. God, this guy was a mystery all right.

"I used to go to voice classes," she replied, "but they were just too expensive, Mam and Dad couldn't afford it anymore, so I gave them up."

"That's tough," Joey replied.

Ann laughed. "Not really, I hated them anyhow. The teacher used to give me the creeps. It was such a relief when Ma told me that I couldn't go anymore. I had to pretend to be disappointed for their sake, but I went to a disco that night to celebrate."

Joey laughed. It was an infectious laugh and soon Ann joined in and any tension between them was broken.

"I didn't think you'd want to join the band after the frosty reception you gave me yesterday when I asked you," Joey said, a smile playing about his lips.

25

"I was in a hurry into town," Ann explained. "I thought the French grind would never finish, there was a bus at 10:30 and if I didn't get it I would have had to wait for another 20 minutes. You held me up, my friend was going mental. I'm sorry if I was abrupt." She smiled, "You were getting on my nerves a little bit."

Joey pointed a finger at himself. "Me? Janey, I put on my sexiest 'Let's get Ann to join our band' smile and all you can say is that I got on your nerves! Thanks a bunch." He put on a wounded look.

Ann giggled, "Go away! I never even noticed your smile."

"Sure that's even more insulting. I bleedin' stayed up all night practising it an' rehearsing what I would say to you an' I got on your nerves. Great." Joey was grinning at her.

Ann noticed with some reluctance that they were outside her house.

"Listen, I have to go," she said smiling. "I'll see you in school tomorrow."

"Sure – see you." Joey smiled in return, as he raised his hand in a farewell gesture.

He began to run then. It was after six and he knew his oul fella would be on the war path if he found that he had gone out.

He was right. His Da shoved him upstairs and told him not to come down again until he had done some studying.

Joey lay down on his bed, plugged in his walkman, unwrapped a bar of chocolate he had bought in the local shop and gave his absent father the two fingers. "Cheers Da," he grinned.

Chapter Four

At seven o'clock the next night, Mick called up to
Joey. "He's upstairs," Mr Boland growled as he let
Mick in. Mick dodged past him and went into Joey's
room.

"God, your Da's in great form," he said as he sat
astride a chair.

"Yeah, he ordered me up here to study," Joey
grinned. "When he came in from work, I was
watchin' the telly and he went mental. He shoved me
up against the wall and yelled in me face. I got a
bleedin' shock. So here I am," he spread his arms
wide, "Slavin' away!"

Mick laughed. Joey had the headphones of his
stereo stuck on his ears, his guitar beside him and
some notes of a song scribbled down on a ragged bit
of paper. Joey indicated the paper. "I'm tryin' to get
into Trev's good books an' write some stuff for the
band," he said.

"You're hard at work all right," Mick commented.
Then he asked, "Listen Joe, I know you'll go mad,
but I got stuck on those Maths again. Can you give
us a hand?"

Joey sighed, "Aw, Mick, do you have to be such a
lick. Where's your Maths book?"

Grinning, Mick got it from his bag. Joey looked
through it. "Which Maths are the ones you can't do?"

"The ones we did in class today."

"What were they? I can't remember. I wasn't really listenin'."

Mick sighed. "How will you know how to do them if you weren't listenin'?" This was hopeless.

"Just tell me what they were."

"Aw, complex numbers or somethin' they were called."

Joey found the chapter and read through it, Mick looking on.

"Janey, Mick," he exclaimed when he'd finished. "I dunno what the hell you're doin' in Honours Maths. The bleedin' things are simple!" He then began to try and explain them to Mick who eventually understood. Joey finished up, to find Mick staring at him.

"What are you lookin' at?" he asked uncomfortably.

"You failed Maths in the Mock," Mick said slowly. "An' yet all you do is read the chapters in the book – no, hang on, you flick through the chapters an' it's as clear as day to you. Me, I could look at the flippin' yoke for days an' never understand it like that. How'd you fail Joe, how?"

"Dunno." Joey studied his fingernails, refusing to look at Mick.

"Sure you don't," Mick scoffed. "I saw you in the Maths exam – you just wrote your name on the top of the page, sat for half an hour and walked out. I thought you'd finished – I couldn't believe it – and then you'd failed, I couldn't believe that either. Joe, what the hell are you playin' at?"

"I'm not playin' at anything," Joey said quietly. "I just don't give a crap about these exams, so can we just drop the subject – right?" He pinned Mick with his stare.

Mick swallowed. Oh oh, he thought. I've stepped over the boundary again. He couldn't understand Joe anymore. There was a time when Joe used to laugh a lot, he was great crack, you could say anything to him and he'd never take offence, but in these past few years, he'd changed. He was still great fun, really popular, but there was something . . . Mick couldn't put his finger on it . . . something deep down, something that had altered Joe from the guy he had been to the guy he was now. You had to tread on thin ice sometimes. It was around the time his Ma had died – he never talked about that either – it had been a weird time.

Joey was smiling in an attempt to change the subject.

"How did you get on with Cathy this mornin'? I saw you run up an' talk to her."

Mick welcomed the peace offer eagerly. He never used to feel uneasy in Joe's presence. "I didn't get too far," Mick confessed. "I walked up to her –"

"Sprinted up to her more likely," Joey interjected.

"All right, sprinted up to her," Mick laughed. "I asked her did she own a pen –"

"Your pen," Joey put in.

Mick nodded. "Yeah, I admit, my pen, and she said, 'no' and continued on walking."

Joey laughed. "An'?"

Mick looked shamefaced. "An' that's it – DA-NA-NA-NA-NA!"

"AW, here," Joey gazed incrediously at his friend. "You mean to say, she said 'nah, that's not my pen' and you just let her get away!"

29

"Sure, what else could I do?" Mick shrugged and spread his hands wide.

"Ask her out, that's what!" Joey said emphatically.

"Oh yeah," Mick retorted scornfully. "So what would you have done?"

Joey considered the question carefully and then in a serious tone he advised Mick to get stinking drunk. "You can do anythin' then!" he stated.

"Yeah, except walk an' talk," Mick laughed.

"Tell you what." Joey jumped off the bed. "We'll go down to The Coach now for a drink and get another dekko at her. I've got some money!" He waved a fiver in Mick's face.

"Thought your Da wants you to study," Mick said doubtfully.

"I'll just tell him I'm goin' over to your house to get a book or somethin'. My Da would swallow a brick – come on."

Mick didn't need to be asked twice. He allowed Joey to drag him downstairs and out of the house.

"Just don't drool inta my pint as well as your own," Joey warned severely as Mick laughed.

Chapter Five

The demo tape was eventually completed at the end of April, four days before the closing date. It consisted of two old songs and two new ones that Joey had written especially for Ann. There was a slow song, "Do You Remember" and a rock song, "Crazy Illusions".

When the final bar of "Crazy Illusions" was played out, the five grinned at each other in delight. "Well, that's it," Trev pronounced as he replayed the Demo tape for them. He began to open a six-pack of beer that he had brought for the occasion and they all had a drink and jokingly toasted their forthcoming success. Mick was given the job of posting the tape and he took it from Trev and reverently placed it in his pocket. They all decided to go to The Nite Spot that Saturday night to celebrate their hard work.

At eight o'clock they left the hall and Mick, Ann and Joey walked home together.

"You doin' anythin' for the weekend?" Mick asked Ann.

She shook her head. "Naw, I'll probably do a bit of studying."

"Janey, no way I'm goin' ta do that!" Joey sounded horrified. "It's a break from school I want, not a reminder."

Changing the subject, Ann asked, "How long have you both been in the band?"

Mick screwed up his face as he considered. "Eh, about five years now." He turned to Joey saying, "Do you remember our first audition, Joe?"

Joey laughed. "Yeah, it was gas."

"Trev had an ad up in one of the local shops, he wanted a guitar player, a drummer an' a keyboard player. So me an' Joe went along, the place was bleedin' packed, *The Commitments* had nothin' on this an' there was Trev in the middle tryin' to organise things, most of the people couldn't play for nuts an' the lead singer Trev had was – what was she Joe?"

"Bleedin' woeful!" Joey confirmed. "She was one of his current girlfriends. When Trev likes someone, he is totally megablind to their flaws. Anyhow, me an' Mick auditioned. We got it but we said that there was no way on earth that we were playing in a band with her singing. So poor old Trev had to choose, he ended up gaining the two of us an' losing a girlfriend. We got a singer then an' she left an' then we ended up with Karen."

"What was so bad about her?" Ann asked.

"Do you wanna tell her?" Mick asked Joey.

Joey grinned. He spread his hands wide saying "She hated my guts, that's what was wrong. You see, me an' Trev used to write the songs for the band, then Trev said that I was better at it an' so it was left to me – I didn't mind cause Trev drove me bananas when we were writing, but Karen went ape. I kept writing stuff she couldn't sing. The notes were too high, the notes were too low, aw, there was always somethin'. She swore I was doin' it on purpose, but I honestly wasn't. I think that was why she left in the end – I drove her to it."

Ann had to smile at the way he said this. He didn't care less that he was responsible for her leaving. "I'd say you miss her."

"Like a bleedin' toothache," Mick replied. "She wrecked all our songs. Joe used to have to alter them all for her, they didn't sound half as nice in the end."

"Where did you do the gigs?"

Joey shrugged. "Anywhere we could get them. We had a good few lined up when Karen left. We sometimes played in The Coach House across the road, we got a few gigs in town an' we even did a mate of Trev's wedding. We had to play other people's stuff for that, but we didn't care, free drink all night, it was cool!"

"I'm surprised you could play at the end of the night," Ann joked.

"No one noticed that we were fairly struggling to hammer out a tune," Mick laughed. "Joe kept missing the cords on the guitar, it was a howl!"

"I was seeing treble, I was so sick the next day, couldn't even get outa the bed."

"Serves you right." They had reached Ann's house and were lingering outside chatting. Just before they left, Ann said hesitantly to Joey, "Mick was telling me that you're great at Maths and I'm a bit stuck on a chapter, would you mind hanging on and explaining something to me?"

Joey's heart sank, but he tried to smile easily. "Yeah, sure. No problem, Ann. Just get the book."

As Ann disappeared up the path, he turned around to Mick to say something but Mick got there first saying, "Fair play to you, I think you're marvellous." Before Joey could retort, he was gone, waving and saying, "I'll see you tomorrow for school, right?"

Chapter Six

Joey began to get impatient. Mick was fifteen minutes late; he was supposed to call at nine o'clock. Chris entered the kitchen then, she was all done up and she had her best clothes on. She kept patting her hair and fluffing it up again. She turned around and regarded her younger brother saying, "Wow, you're all done up, baby bruv – where are you going?"

"Out," replied Joey, looking at his watch again.

"Out where?" Chris persisted.

"The Nite Spot."

"See you there so," Chris laughed as Joey groaned with dismay. The last time he had been there, he had been with this girl and his sister had come over and pretended to be his girlfriend. There had been war and all Joey's mates had slagged him about it for ages.

Just then, the doorbell rang and Chris ran to answer it. Her face fell when she saw it was only Mick. He took her hand and kissed it saying, "Aw, Chris, you didn't have to dress up for me, you know I always think you look ravishing."

Chris laughed. "Sorry, Mick you're out of luck this evening, I've got a date, but I might be able to squeeze you in for a slow dance if you book me early enough."

34

"Consider yourself booked so."

Laughing, Chrystal went upstairs as Mick turned towards Joey, who exclaimed, "Where the hell have you been?"

Mick plonked himself down on a chair as he said, "We don't have to rush. Trev has his Da's car for the night, so he is pickin' us up. Sorry I didn't phone you but he only rang me a few minutes ago."

"Do you want a cuppa while we're waitin'?"

Outside, there was the sound of a car-horn blaring. "That's Trev," Mick said. "I told him to blow the horn twice when he came."

Domo waved at them. "There's going to be a squash, there'll be five in the back seat."

"Sure, Mick can sit on my knee," Joey laughed.

Mick shook his head. "No way, I wouldn't trust you."

Eventually, Mick, Joey, Ann, and two of Ann's friends, Betty and Hazel, were piled uncomfortably in the back.

"Now," Domo waved some papers about in the air, "on a happy note . . ."

"Dong," came the reply from Mick which was received with the usual groans this joke received every time he managed to slip it in.

"As I was sayin'," Domo continued, "I got seven free passes for this evening. A guy in work is a part-time barman up there, he gave them to me."

The others were delighted. The disco was expensive, especially on a Saturday night, so to get in free was great.

When Trev had parked the car, they got out and joined the queue. The place was going to be packed. Domo gave them a pass each, which they showed at

35

the door. They handed their coats into the cloakroom and wandered into the disco.

"Janey!" Ann exclaimed. "There'll be no hope of seeing anyone from school in this crowd."

"Let's find an obscure table," Joey said to Mick. "I don't want Chris to spot me at all."

Unfortunately, the only free tables left were at the edge of the dance floor and reluctantly Joey agreed to sit there.

"OK, what's everyone havin'?" he asked. "I've cash tonight for a change." He pulled a rather crumpled £20 note from his pocket, that he had got for baby-sitting his cousin. After they had all told him what they wanted, he asked Mick to come and help him carry the drinks back to the table.

"Hate to be the one to tell you this, Joe, but Laura Peters has just plonked herself down beside your seat."

Joey sighed. "Yeah, I noticed," he said mournfully. "She's lovely lookin' but terrible stupid. I wouldn't say there's a lot between her ears. What do you think, Mick?"

As there was no reply, Joey repeated himself. Still no reply, so turning around, Joey went to say it a third time. Mick was no where in sight. "Wha' the –" Joey's face broke into a grin. Mick was stalking some blond girl – it could only be Cathy. "Headcase," Joey said to himself as he shook his head in disbelief. Janey, Mick had it bad. He lost sight of his friend then, so he continued on toward the bar.

Mick still hadn't returned when he got back. He had borrowed a tray from the bar, on the promise that he would return it.

"Where did Mick get to?" Domo asked.

Joey proceeded to tell them and they all began to laugh.

"You're not serious," Betty said. "My God, that's gas!"

They were still laughing when Mick returned. "Sorry about that," he said ruefully. "But I wanted to find out where she was sitting."

"Forget it." Joey pushed a pint toward him. "Here, drink up. You'll need it before the night is over."

Mick grinned, saying "The way Laura is lookin' at you, I won't be the only one."

"She's not my type," Joey replied as Mick, lifting his drink uttered a scornful, "Yeah, sure."

The slow sets came on around midnight. Mick gulped down his pint, took a deep breath and left the table. Joey watched him go and tried not to laugh. He was glad he hadn't made fun of him when Mick arrived back about two minutes later looking very glum indeed. Mick plonked himself down next to Ann who looked at him questioningly.

"What's the story?" Joey asked as Mick glowered into his pint.

"Aw, I went to ask Cathy for a dance an' she told me her boyfriend was up at the bar, buyin' a drink."

"Oh, oh." Joey felt sorry for Mick.

Mick attempted to smile. "Sure, the best ones are always taken."

"Maybe they'll break up – eh, Micko?" Joey laughed.

"THAT'S AWFUL!" Ann exclaimed, trying to suppress a smile.

"No it's not, I hope they do too," Mick agreed.

"Where's she sittin'?" Joey asked standing up. "I'll go an' get a dekko at the competition."

"No you bleedin' won't," an alarmed Mick pulled him down. "What are you havin'? I'm goin' to the bar."

Mick left and Joey got up. "Don't tell him where I am if he gets back before me," he said grinning at Ann, as she said, "He'll go mental if he finds out."

He hadn't gone far when a voice said, "Joe, I didn't know you were coming up here tonight, thanks for telling me."

Joey spun round. A girl from school stood there. "Amy, how's it goin'? I'm just up here with the lads from the band."

"Well, you might as well say 'Hi' to the rest of us – we're all sitting over here." She put her hand on his arm and steered him through the crowd.

Upon reaching Amy's table, Joey's eyes lit up. Cathy and her friends were at the very next table. This was a stroke of luck.

He made small talk to his mates, who were getting slowly jarred, before moving over to Cathy. He sat beside her and said, "Hiya Cathy!"

She and her friend turned to him, unable to believe that some guy they didn't know from Adam had just encroached upon their conversation. Joey gave them both a winning smile. "It is Cathy – isn't it?"

"Yes," she answered coolly, her eyes appraising this hunk in front of her. "May we have the pleasure of your name?" Her voice dripped with sarcasm.

"Yep," Joey was undeterred. "It's Joe – Joe Boland. You work in The Coach, don't you?" Again the charming smile.

Cathy was beginning to smile now. "Yes, I do. Oh, hang on, I do know you. I've served you a few times in there, you and your mates . . ." her voice trailed away.

"One of my mates asked you to dance a while ago." Joey decided to strike while the iron was hot. He had never intended to do this, it was juvenile, but sure what could he lose – except his front teeth when Mick found out, he thought wryly.

"So?" Cathy was frosty again.

"So you told him you had a boyfriend an' I don't seem to see him around." Joey made a big deal of looking. "Where is he?"

Cathy shook her head in disbelief. "What business is it of yours?" she asked increduously.

Joey shrugged. "None, none at all. But that doesn't take from the fact that you lied."

"What is this?" Cathy burst out. "Some kinda 'Joe's Matchmaker Service'? Does your friend get you to do this all the time?"

"Yeah – the pay's great." Joey joked and then he said, "He doesn't know I'm here. He'd flip if I told him what I've just said. I can't even believe that I'm doing this myself."

"Neither can I," Cathy mumbled.

"I'm just askin' you to give him a chance, he thinks you're great." Joey bit his lip. This was stupid, the girl must think he was crazy. He got up to go when Cathy said, "I don't like dancin' with strange fellas at discos. They only want the one thing."

"Sure there's no harm in hopin'," Joey smiled and then he said, "Mick wouldn't do anything like that anyhow, just give him a chance – you've nothin' to lose."

"Go on, Cath," her friend urged, thinking how romantic all this was.

"All right," Cathy said in a not too gracious manner. "But he had better not try anything on."

"I'll try an' get him over to you in the next set of slows. I'll sellotape his lips together."

Cathy's friend gave a giggle at this but Cathy wasn't one bit amused. "Right," she said glumly. "One chance."

Mick was mortified. "You did what?" he asked again.

"Just forget it." Joey was trying his best not to laugh. "Haven't you got what you wanted?"

"OH WOW!" Mick said, annoyed. "Only 'cause you decide to play matchmaker. Aw Joe, it's so bleedin' embarrassing. What kinda thick does she think I am – getting you to go over to her. Well, you can feck off if you think I'm facing her after this! Jaysus, how could I? Aw God, Joe, I can't believe you did it!" He sank his head into his hands and gave a deep sigh, saying again weakly "I cannot believe you went over there an'. . ."

"Yeah well, you'd better believe it," Joey said mildly. "An' if you don't ask her to dance in the next set of slows, she'll have an even worse opinion of you than she does already."

"Oh great choice!" Mick groaned. He looked at his watch. They usually played a slow set every hour. The next would be at one o'clock. He had thirty minutes to make up his mind about what he was going to do.

Mick's heart gave a lurch as "Orchard Road" boomed out. Joey, who was well on at this stage, gave him a shove. "Go on, Mick, dazzle her with your charm," he laughed.

"I could kill you, Joe," he said viciously, as to the whoops and cheers of the others, he tried to make a dignified approach to Cathy's table.

40

Joey found himself alone after about ten minutes. He vaguely wondered how Mick was getting on. He hadn't come back anyhow and that was a good sign.

"Now," crooned the DJ "Let's slow it right down!" The lights dimmed as "Something in the Air Tonight" began to play. Couples slowly drifted toward the dance floor and began to dance in each other's arms. Joey drained his third pint and began to fumble in his pocket for more money. He saw Trev busy chatting up a blond in a black mini. Domo was dancing with his ex – Carla. Everyone, it seemed, was dancing with someone. The song ended and "Romeo and Juliet" was put on. Joey loved this song. "Ladies' choice this time," the DJ announced. "Come on, girls, don't be shy, ask that fella to dance!"

Joey stood up, ready to go to the bar, when from behind a voice said, "Well, Joe, do you want to dance?" Laura smiled charmingly as Joey began to sweat. He didn't want to refuse her and hurt her feelings, but the girl was suffocating him. She was the most forceful girl he had ever met.

He managed to grin. "Sure." He took her hand and led her onto the dance floor. He put his hands lightly on her hips as she twined her arms around his neck. "Great song – huh?" Joey was at a loss for things to say. He was busy trying to keep his distance from her.

Laura nodded. "Yeah, who sings it?"

"Dire Straits," Joey answered.

"Never heard of them," Laura said dismissively. She attempted to get closer to him. She put her head against his chest. Joey's head was spinning. What the hell was he supposed to do? He was into one night stands, but not with someone he was likely to meet

41

again. Anyhow, the way Laura was going she obviously wanted more from him than a casual kiss and cuddle at a disco. Joey hated the idea of getting involved in a relationship. He would feel trapped; he didn't like the idea of always being with the one person. He had never bothered going out with anyone and he was damned if he was going to start now.

Laura was moving closer by the second. Joey felt his arms tighten about her for an instant, as he smelt the sweet scent of her hair . . .

"Bitch!" Laura was yanked from his arms and thrown onto the floor. "How dare you." A tall lanky youth with greasy hair was standing over Laura and yelling into her face.

"Hey," Joey attempted to intervene and it was then the youth turned to him. Recognition dawned in both lads' faces at the same time.

"Bloody Boland," Jim Kendell spat. He jabbed a finger into Joey's chest. "Leave – her – alone – she's – mine. I'll bleedin' kill you."

Joey's eyes filled with scorn. Jim Kendell had been in school with him. He had succeeded in getting expelled in third year, before he even sat his Junior Cert. Rumours abounded as to what he was doing now. Grabbing Kendell by the shirt Joey hissed, "I can feckin' dance with whoever I like an' you ever feckin' treat a girl like that again and I will kill you." Turning to Laura, who was sobbing quietly, he asked gruffly, "Are you OK?"

She nodded and was led away by one of her friends. Kendell tried to go after her, but was stopped by two bouncers. They proceeded to drag him off the dance-floor. He spat and swore all the way off that he was going to "do" Joey.

Joey just grinned and waved as he was led away. Inside he was shaking, but he wouldn't let Kendell see it.

The guy was a headcase – full of shit.

He made his way back to the table only to notice that not one of his mates had seen the commotion. They were eager to hear the story and Joey, a born story-teller, was only too glad to oblige them. He made it more thrilling with each retelling.

Joey got in at about three in the morning. He tried to be as quiet as possible. There was no point in annoying his Da by being too noisy. He'd be like an anti-Christ if he was woken up.

Joey grinned as he closed the front door gently behind him. It had been a great night. Laura was off his back – she had tearfully apologised to him for Kendell's behaviour. Then, with a dreamy look in her eyes that totally shocked Joey she had announced proudly that Kendell was a bit possessive.

The girl was mad – Joey was convinced of it.

Mick had a date with Cathy and was in great form. Domo was back with the irritating Carla. Yeah, it had been great.

Returning to the present, Joey saw that the light was on in the kitchen. He heard Chris's voice and decided to join her. She was probably having tea with Gerry. "How's it goin'?" he said loudly, as he opened the kitchen door. Four faces looked at him. There was his Da, Dee, Chris and some stranger that he didn't know. They all smiled at him, even his Da, which he thought was odd.

"You must smell grub," Dee remarked as she got a cup down from the press for him.

"Disco was good, wasn't it?" Chris said.

"Feckin' great," Joey replied enthustically, as he waited for Dee to introduce him to her friend. The woman was not the sort of person you would expect Dee to hang round with, he thought. She was about forty, tall, slim and elegant looking, bits of grey in her hair.

To Joey's surprise and horror, his Da stood up and with his hand resting lightly on the woman's shoulder he said, "Irene, I'd like you to meet Joe. Joe, this is Irene."

Joey stopped eating. He looked in confusion from his Da to this woman. He had thought that she was one of his sister's friends, never his Da's, never!

"Nice to meet you, Joey." Irene held out her hand. Her accent was cultured.

Joey stared dumbly at her. This was a sick joke! How could his Da do this? It was digusting! How the hell could he go out with someone else? How could he bring her to his home? Joey's mind whirled.

Slowly Irene's hand descended. She flushed. There was an uncomfortable silence.

"Joe," his father cut in on his thoughts. "Where's your manners?"

Joey gazed in disbelief at his Da. He looked at his two sisters who had been chatting happily to this stranger. He put his cup down on the table. Straightening himself up he said, "If you'll all excuse me, I'm goin' to bed."

He walked out of the kitchen, leaving four open mouths behind him. His mind swirled, his thoughts reeled and he was convinced that he was going to puke.

Chapter Seven

Mr Boland burst into the kitchen that Easter Sunday morning and storming up to Joey yelled, "Don't you ever, ever insult a friend of mine the way you did last night!" His Da's finger was nearly jabbing his eye out. "DO YOU HEAR ME? DO YOU HEAR ME!"

"Loud an' clear." Joey's voice was insolent and mocking. He moved away from his father and began to peel the potatoes for lunch.

"You upset her – do you know that?" His Da was directly behind him, breathing into his ear.

"I really couldn't give a damn about your fancy woman's feelings."

They were eyeball to eyeball, nose to nose.

"How dare you use that term about her – how dare you!" Mr Boland grabbed a handful of his son's shirt. "God, Joe," he breathed. "Don't make me hit you. I've never hit any of my kids, never. But I don't know how I stop with you – I really don't." He tried to force his hands from becoming fists.

Joey stared at him and said with perfect composure, "She is your fancy woman. You bleedin' put your arm on her shoulder, she holds your hand. What the hell else would you call her – huh?"

"She is my lady friend! She is a lovely woman and you have no right to upset her."

Joey tore himself out of his father's grasp. He

45

stood in front of his Da, his eyes blazing. "I WILL NOT BE NICE TO ANYONE WHO COMES IN HERE TRYIN' TO REPLACE ME MA." His voice faltered. He began to back out of the room saying, "No way, Da, you can forget it."

Mr Boland reeled back. He felt that he had been dealt a body blow. This was the first time that Joe had mentioned his mother in three years. "She is not trying to take Marie's place, Joe," he said softly.

Joey stared at him, his eyes were wild with confusion. He swallowed and said equally softly, "I hope you remember that, Da, when you're out with her, an' talkin' to her, an' holdin' her hand. I hope you remember you bleedin' said that." He turned on his heel and left the kitchen. He couldn't trust himself to say any more.

Pete Boland took up the knife his son had flung down and began to finish off the spuds. He couldn't see for the tears that blurred his eyes. He sat down in a chair and tried to compose himself. "He mentioned her," he half whispered. "After three years he mentioned her. He hasn't forgotten her. Oh, thank you, God – thank you!"

"Joe in?" Mick thought that Joe's Da looked pretty strange today. His eyes looked sore or something.

"Upstairs."

He was being kinda gruff too. Mick didn't linger. Dodging past him, he was soon hammering up the stairs. He burst into Joey's room. "Guess what, Boland?"

"Wha'?" Joey was uninterested.

"REM are signing copies of their CD in HMV today – do you want to come in?"

46

"No," Joey said rudely, not even looking at Mick.

Mick wasn't the least bit discouraged. "Aw, come on Joe. It'll be a bit of crack."

Joey sighed heavily and turning bored eyes upon his friend he said, "I'm not in the humour for crack."

Mick grinned. "Oh yeah, you get some kinda personality operation during the night or wha'?" He plonked himself down on Joey's bed as he continued, "Hang on – I bet you it's Kendell – he scared the shit out of you last night an' now you're afraid to go out the door?"

Joey had to smile at this. "Shakin' in me shoes," he joked as he lifted himself up on his elbow.

"Come on Joe," Mick coaxed. "I promise – no crack – fingers crossed. It'll be just a dull borin' trip into town."

"So what's new?" Joey laughed as Mick pulled a face. "I'll get me jacket." He went to the wardrobe and rummaged through it. He eventually found his jacket among the clothes on the floor. "Thought it was hung up," he said as he shook it out.

Mick stifled a grin. Joey was notoriously untidy, scatty and laid back.

After the jacket, Joey had to search for money. He found some in his dustbin. He grinned ruefully at Mick. He shrugged, saying, "I could've sworn I put it in me jacket." The money was then painstakingly sellotaped together. "I musta torn it by accident." Mick just laughed at this and Joey gave him a puzzled look. Mick merely indicated his watch as he said urgently, "Come on Joe, it's gettin' late. We better hurry."

On the way into town, Joey was quiet and preoccupied. Mick thought of asking him what the matter was, but as usual he chickened out. It was hard to tell what way Joe would take it. I'm not takin' a risk like that other time, he thought, No way – not again.

It was over chips in McDonald's that Joey suddenly blurted out, "He has a girlfriend."

"Wha'? Who?"

Joey immediately wished that he had kept his mouth shut. He shrugged. "Aw – no one – forget it!"

Mick was curious. "Go on Joe, who has a girlfriend? What's the big secret?"

Joey gazed down at the table. He squashed the plastic cup between his fingers. "No secret," he said trying to be casual, but still unable to look at Mick. Then he said, in a more uneven tone of voice, "Me Da has."

Mick nearly choked. He began to cough violently after spitting his Coke back into his cup. "No shit! Your Da has a girlfriend?!" Disbelief was written all over his face and it echoed in his voice. So that's what's buggin' him, he thought.

Joey nodded miserably. "She was there when I went home last night – imagine me Da havin' someone else – it's bleedin' digusting."

"What's she like?" Mick was agog. Joey's oul fella – well there was hope for anyone so!

Joey shrugged. "I didn't really look at her. I wouldn't talk to her. I told me Da not to expect me to neither."

"Maybe it won't last," Mick tried to say by way of consolation.

"When she gets to know me Da she'll dump him!" Joey grinned weakly, as he took a chip from Mick's portion.

"That's me boy!" Mick laughed, hoping that Joe was right. He didn't think that Joe would be able to take it, if his Da started hanging around with other women.

Changing the subject, before Mick could say any more, Joey asked, "How did you get on with the Maths in the end?"

Mick groaned. "Don't remind me, I wouldn't have got them done if you hadn't helped me. It depresses me to even think about it."

"Haven't you little to be depressed about," Joey replied, as he drained his Coke. "Look at me – failed all me subjects."

At this, Mick unable to restrain himself, exploded, "Yeah Joe, sure you did. Failed 'em all deliberately, you mean!" He was surprised at the anger in his voice.

Joey was surprised as well. "Huh?" he said in disbelief.

"Don't look so surprised," Mick said, a slight edge of sarcasm in his voice. "It's so obvious. You are bleedin' brilliant, I mean *really* brilliant and you fail everything in the Mock – no way Joe – no bleedin' way!"

Joey said nothing. He would not look at Mick.

"I dunno why you did it Joe. Maybe you wanted your oul fella to think you were useless an' let you play music instead – I dunno." Mick leaned over the table at him as he went on, "But one thing I do know Joe, is that you are bleedin' mad. You could get As all over the place, it's such a waste. I would love to be like that. You make me mad, so you do!" Mick was so annoyed, he didn't care less what Joe would say. It was about time someone said something to him.

Joey had never seen his mate like this. Jokingly, to ease the situation, he said, "Tell you what, I'll give you grinds in all the subjects if you want."

To his horror, Mick's face lit up. "Would you? Would you, Joe? That'd be great. Are you serious?"

"Eh –"

"Great, thanks. Tell you what, come over to my house every weeknight an' give us a hand, would you?"

Joey nearly died. "Eh –"

"Thanks, Joe. That'd be brilliant!"

"Only for an hour or so, right?" Joey decided to get this in quickly. He did not want to spend all his nights slaving away over schoolwork.

"Sure – great!" Mick began to pull on his jacket. "Thanks Joe, that's great!"

"Yeah," Joey replied ruefully. "I really am glad I came into town with you today."

Chapter Eight

Saturday afternoon in mid-May, and Joey awoke
with a thumping headache. He had been helping
Mick with study for the past few weeks and for a
surprise Mick had brought him out drinking last
night. He groaned as he turned over to look at his
alarm clock. "Shite," he exclaimed, jumping up in
shock. It was mid-day. He had to steady himself – he
didn't think that he had drunk all that much last
night, but obviously it had been sufficient to give
him a hangover. He had a feeling that his Da would
eat him out of it later. Grinning, he remembered the
look on his Da's face as he had barged into the
kitchen last night. His Da had been in there with
Irene and he, Joe, had given a mock bow saying,
"Excuse me" in as slurred a voice as he could muster.

"Get out, you're drunk," his Da had snarled.

Joey had got out, sobering slightly at seeing his
Da's arm resting protectively on *her* shoulder.

Joey threw on some clothes at breakneck speed.
Pulling his shapeless Aran jumper over his head, he
took the stairs two at a time.

He went into the kitchen to get some grub, that
was if his stomach could stand it. He took two
painkillers before putting on the kettle.

It was then he heard the ponderous footsteps from

51

the sitting-room. His Da was making his way out to the kitchen and Joey groaned inwardly. Trust his Da to pick a time when he was at his queasiest.

Joey knew by his father's stride that things were going to be rough. He swallowed, determined to stand his ground.

His father was two feet from him and going pretty red in the face. Joey tried to look as if he didn't care.

"I am just warning you," Mr Boland said in a low dangerous voice, "That no son and I mean NO SON OF MINE will ever come into MY house and make a spectacle of themselves in the way you did last night, you got that?"

"Huh – if yer woman hadn't been there, you wouldn't have cared." The words were out before Joey could stop them.

"If Irene hadn't been there, SONNY BOY, there would be pieces of you all over the kitchen this morning. I was so ashamed of you last night – imagine, being ashamed of my own son!"

"I don't give a shit what you think of me," Joey said, knowing as he did so that it was a lie.

The words were like a knife in Mr Boland's gut. His hurt made him want to strike back, as, jabbing his son in the chest with his finger, he said, "Just as well, how could I ever be proud of you – a guitar-playing freak – that's all you are."

Joey suddenly found himself unable to speak. There was a huge lump in his throat. He stared dumbly at his father with huge dazed eyes. He wanted to scream, to yell, to hurt him, but he couldn't.

Mr Boland knew he had gone too far, but the kid deserved it. He turned from him saying, "Just get out of my sight, go on! Go and study or do something useful for God's sake!"

Joey stayed rooted to the spot. The words "guitar-playing freak" bounded and rebounded inside his head. It hurt so much! He felt anger bubbling up from inside, pushing his hurt to the back of his mind. His Da turned around once more and yelled, "GO ON – MOVE, CAN'T YA!"

As if in a dream, from far away, Joey heard himself say, "Fuck you!" He watched, unconcerned, as his father's eyes widened in surprise.

"What did you say?" Incredulity in his Da's voice.

"Are you deaf? I said 'Fuck you!'" Joey's voice had risen a pitch. He was sailing close to a storm, but he really didn't care. His Da's fist caught him unprepared. He was smashed against the door, his right eye searing in pain. He held his face in his hand and ducked defensively as his Da grabbed him by his sweatshirt and dragged him upright. Mr Boland was horrified at the state of his son's eye. He hadn't meant to do damage like that, he had thought the eejit would duck! But to show remorse now would weaken his position. He shook his son like a rat, saying all the while, "You never, ever talk to me like that again." He poked his face into to his son's, as the control he'd exercised for years, where Joe was concerned, abandoned him. "You just apologise to me at once – NOW!"

Joey regarded him with contempt. "Piss off!" For this, his head was slammed back against the door, his eye a hammer blast of pain.

"You didn't hear me, I think." Mr Boland's voice was low and quivering with rage. "I think I demanded an apology and I didn't get one. Say you're sorry."

Joey bit his lip, his eyes insolent.

"SAY YOU'RE SORRY!"

Joey shrugged indifferently. "You insulted me first Da an' you didn't apologise, so you can bleedin' wait for your apology cause you won't get it from me!"

"SAY YOU'RE SORRY!"

"You insulted me first."

"Give me an apology!" He was shaking him again.

"No," Joey calmy replied as once more his head was banged against the door. He attempted to shove his Da off him and this seemed to infuriate Mr Boland further. He threw Joey across the kitchen and began to advance on him. Joey, fists clenched, stood his ground, his heart pounding, feeling slightly sickened.

The kitchen door was burst open. "STOP IT, STOP IT, BOTH OF YOU!" Dee yelled, placing herself between them. "Dad, what are you doing? Leave him alone, please!" Her voice broke as she tried to stifle back tears. Mr Boland gulped as he stared at his son. He looked down at his hands, as if he could not quite believe that he had used them to hit Joey. He turned them over as if in a daze. He swallowed, "Jesus, I . . ."

"Your eye, Joe." Dee was concerned, she went to touch it, but he pulled away muttering, "Leave it. It's OK. I said leave it, Dee."

"What the hell is all this about?" Dee gazed at the two of them, concern written all over her face. "Da?"

Mr Boland coughed. He was horrified. Had he really done that to Joe's eye? God knew, the lad had a wallop coming, but that . . . "Well," he began uncertainly, "he told me –"

Joey pushed past both of them muttering, "I'm goin' out."

"Joe, we have to talk," his father pleaded, as the door slammed shut. His shoulders slumped and Dee's heart went out to him. "I never meant to catch his eye like that Dee, it was an accident. I only told him not to come in drunk – we traded a few insults," he laughed bitterly, "no different to normal, and then the fecker tells me to F off." He rubbed his face with a shaky hand. "God, I could have killed him, Dee. He made me see red. I've never hit any of my kids, ever, and look at what he made me do!" He sank into a chair and covered his face with his hands. Dee stood awkwardly by, not knowing what to do. Eventually, she put her hand on his shoulder, saying, "Come on, Da, forget it. Talk to him when he gets back. You know Joe, he's never in bad form for long."

Joey walked aimlessly, thinking nothing, his head well down and his eye throbbing like mad. He was surprised when he found himself outside Marley Park. He went in and found a quiet spot where he could think. He felt slightly sick and his heart was pumping. He sat down on a bench and closed his eyes.

"How's it goin'?"

Joey jumped at the cheery greeting. Just when he didn't need to meet anyone. "Hiya, Ann," he mumbled, looking away from her.

"What are you doing here at this hour?" she asked, plonking herself down beside him.

Joey shrugged. "Just fancied a walk. It's a nice day."

"Me too."

There was an awkward silence. Ann gulped and said somewhat uncomfortably, "Do you not want me here?"

The direct question caught Joey unawares. He turned to her exclaiming, "Sorry, I didn't mean to . . ." He didn't finish as Ann was staring in horror at his eye.

"What happened?" she exclaimed loudly.

Joey shrugged and turned away from her saying, "Aw, nothin'."

55

Ann gave a nervous laugh. "Joey, have you seen your eye? It's huge! You'd better go home and put some ice on it."

"Yeah," Joey said indifferently.

"What'll your Da say when he sees it – will he give you the third degree?"

Joey gave an ironic laugh. "Hardly likely, seein' as he's the one that's responsible for it!" As soon as he spoke, Joey wished that he had kept his mouth shut. Ann looked horrified, she probably thought that his Da was a child beater or somethin'.

"We had a row," he hastened to explain. "I told him to f – off and voilà." He pointed to his face.

"Wow," Ann breathed. "He must've been really mad."

"He was," Joey said ruefully. "We don't really get on too well."

"No?"

"Nah." Joey bit his lip. He tried to keep his voice calm and normal. It was hard to talk about. "He thinks I'm a bit of a waster actually."

Ann gulped uncomfortably. "Look, Joe," she ventured, "If you want me to go, I will. If you want to talk, it won't go any further, I promise."

Joey shrugged, he tried to say in as level as voice as possible, "Nothin' to tell really. We just don't see eye to eye – if you'll pardon the pun – we never have. This is the first time he's hit me . . ." he stopped and said almost to himself in a bitter, angry voice, "an' the bleedin' last!"

Ann said nothing. She didn't know whether to stay or go. There was silence for a few minutes and then Joey said quietly, out of the blue, "It all started when she died."

"Who?" Ann asked. "When who died?"

"Me Ma." He was tearing leaves from a tree growing beside the seat. He carefully folded the leaves in half and in half again and then tearing them he let the wind take them from his palm.

"She kept us apart, me an' me Da. She never let us fight. She was music mad too, you see. She let me play whenever I wanted. She was a great musician," his voice swelled with pride. "She won loadsa scholarships an' stuff – she threw the whole lot up when she married Da. Imagine doin' that – she must've been mad." Joey stopped. He rubbed his hand over his face distractedly. "Mad," he said again softly.

Still, Ann made no comment. She didn't think Joe wanted her to.

"Me Da used to indulge her, he let me do what I wanted when she was around. When she . . . when she . . . you know, got sick an' . . . an' died, he changed his tune. I was sixteen, doin' me Junior Cert an' he kept tellin' me to study. He said she would have wanted me to do well. I wrote music most of the time, but I studied a bit as well, to keep him happy. I got As all over the place."

Ann, despite herself, gasped and Joey grinned for the first time. "It was a cinch." Bitterness crept into his voice as he continued, "Me Da was so proud. Proud of his bleedin' 'straight A' son. I won a competition a few weeks later for songwritin'. He didn't give a shit, all he could talk about was how well I was likely to do in the Leavin'." He paused and a small smile flickered across his face. "I began to deliberately fail all my exams. I got Es an' everything in the Mock. It drove him feckin' mad. It was bleedin' great!" He turned to Ann grinning.

She was unable to smile back. "But Joe –"

He brushed her off. "Don't you start," he said in a

57

sulky voice. "I get enough grief from Mick. I want to be liked for myself, not 'cause I get great Leaving Cert results! Can't you understand that?"

The last sentence was a plea and Ann's heart went out to him. She lightly touched his sleeve saying, "I do Joe, honest."

"He flippin' hates the band. I can't even talk about it to him. If I play a song or practise or anythin', I have to tell him Mick writes the stuff – he'd go mental if he thought I was in me bedroom writin' songs instead of studyin'."

Joey paused and then continued angrily, "He laughs when I tell him I want to be a musician – he laughs! If I said that I wanted to be a doctor or . . . or an accountant like him he'd be delighted. He'd tell all his mates about me."

Ann swallowed and said nervously, "Joe, don't get mad at me for saying this, will you?"

At once she saw his face become guarded. "What?"

She gulped. "Would it be so bad for you to do well in the Leaving?"

Joey looked incredulously at her. "I spend the last ten minutes telling you why I can't do well in the Leavin' and this is all you can say." He got up to leave adding, "Thanks a bunch, Ann."

"Oh, for God's sake," Ann snapped. "Will you stop behaving so childishly. Sit down and listen to my proposal, at least."

Joey was stunned at her outburst. He stood above her, hands in his jean pockets. He quirked an eyebrow and shrugged. "OK, I'll listen." He did not sit down.

"Do well in the Leaving to keep the peace at home, and when your Da asks you what you are going to do, tell him that you are going to write music and he can like it or lump it!"

"That's no good, sure the rows would start again."

"Just tell your Da that if the music doesn't work out for you, you can always fall back on your Leaving Cert." She looked at him expectantly. "Well, would that work?"

"I suppose I could give it a try," Joey said without much enthusiasm. "But it just seems like me Da is getting his way."

"You'll get your way too," Ann pointed out reasonably. "And you'll get it without fighting with everyone."

Joey grinned. "I don't fight with everyone, just me Da." He sat down beside Ann then saying, "I guess you're right. I'll give it a go anyhow. It'll be so borin' studyin' – I'll hate it."

"So join the rest of the world," Ann said matter-of-factly. "Get real, Joe. No one likes studying."

"Ooh, that's me rightly put in me box," Joey laughed. "Thanks Ann, you're great." He gave her a dazzling smile and she blushed.

"For what?" she asked awkwardly.

"For listenin'," Joey said simply. "I don't ever really talk about me Ma an' stuff . . . sorry for borin' you, but thanks."

Ann shrugged, still red-faced. "I didn't mind."

Joey got up from the seat and brushed the leaves from his jeans. He held out his hand to her saying, "You comin'? – it's gettin' late, let's walk back to the entrance."

Ann allowed him to haul her from the seat. She dropped his hand immediately to brush down her own jeans. "Keep your head well down," she joked. "I don't want people thinking I belted you one."

Chapter Nine

"JOE!" Chris yelled. When he made no reply she yelled even louder, "JOE!"

"Yeah?" He looked down over the banister, his face a mask of boredom. He had taken Ann's advice and was now doing a little study. It was less than two weeks to the Leaving. He was absolutely fed up. He did realise, however, that Ann was right and he was glad that he had confided in her.

Chris looked at him in exasperation. "Do you ever answer when someone calls?" she demanded, and before waiting for his reply she said, "There's a call for you." She stalked back into the kitchen.

Joey hadn't even heard the phone ring. He bounded down the stairs and picked up the receiver. "Yeah?"

"Hiya, Joe, it's Mick." His voice sounded breathless.

"How's it goin'? What's the story?" Joey asked, his curiosity aroused. Then reluctantly he asked, "You're not after a hand with the Maths or anythin' are you?"

He was greatly relieved when Mick began to laugh. "Naw, Joe," and then in the same breathless voice, he announced importantly, "You won't believe what I have to tell you – two bits of bleedin' great news."

Joey's heart quickened. He didn't want to hope –
"Is it to do with the demo tape?" he asked dubiously.

"Yeah." Mick was grinning, Joey could tell. "I only
posted it a few weeks ago, an'," Mick paused and
then yelled, "WE DID IT JOE! WE'RE INTA THE
SECOND ROUND!" He was shouting so loudly,
Joey had to hold the phone away from his ear. He
could hear Mick's Ma givin' out yards to him for
yelling. Mick took no notice. "Well, isn't it cool, Joe?

"It's flippin' brilliant, so it is." Joey had to stop
himself from shouting. If his Da heard about the
band being in a competition, there would be war. He
felt a pang of regret that he couldn't share his news
with anyone – Chris and Dee would be sure to tell
his Da and he didn't want that. "How'd you find
out?" he asked Mick, who at this stage was having a
heated argument with his mother at the other end of
the phone.

"Hang on a sec, Joe." The phone was put down
and Joey grinned as he heard Mick say, "Look, Ma, I
can't help it if your reaction to good news is different
to mine – can I? I don't yell at you when you bawl
your eyes out, do I?"

The phone was picked up a few seconds later.
"Sorry 'bout that – what did you ask me just before I
had to, eh, sort me Ma out."

Joe grinned. "I just wanted to know how you
found out about us gettin' through."

"Trev rang me – he thought that I'd probably like
to tell you myself. At least you can tell yer oul fella
about getting into the second round of this
competition. He'll probably be delighted for you.
He'll hardly slag off the band now."

Joey laughed. "Sure, sure he'd be delighted,

Mick," he said sarcastically. "Anyhow, I'm not talkin' to him. He can feck off. He didn't apologise for givin' me that black eye so he can just feck off!"

"Aw, Joe, he has tried to talk to you since, you told me so yourself." Mick had been shocked to hear that Joe's Dad had belted him. He was even more shocked when he had seen the results of the belt. Joe hadn't told him the full story, only that there had been a row of some sort and that his Da had hit him. He had made him promise not to tell anyone else and so they had told the lads in school that Joey had fought off a would-be pick-pocket. Everyone in school had clapped Joe on the back and told him how brave he was. He and Joe had had a great laugh.

"Look, Mick, let's forget about me Da. I am not talkin' to him an' that's the end of it."

There was an uncomfortable silence.

"You're like an oul' one naggin' me," Joey continued, in a jocular voice. "I think you take after your ma."

Mick still said nothing.

"Aw, come on Mick, it was just a joke."

"Yeah, the way you always joke when someone says somethin' too close to the bone," Mick exploded.

This time it was Joey's turn to go silent.

"I can't see the reason for you not talkin' to your Da. I'm sure you did as much shoutin' as he did. Don't take the flippin' head off me cause I tell you what I think an' then turn it into a joke, Joe. I am sick of you doin' that!"

"I don't –"

"You *do*," Mick was really irked at him.

"Who the hell rattled your cage?" Joey asked

bewildered. "Sorry for whatever I did. I'm still not talkin' to me Da though."

"Fine," Mick sighed. "Forget I spoke."

"Forgotten," Joey replied and then, "Listen Mick, you'll never guess what I was doin' when you called!"

"What?" Mick said in a pretty fed-up voice.

"Studyin'! Da-na-na-nah."

"'bout time." Mick was not a bit amused.

"Gee-sus, come on Mick. I said I'm sorry. Don't you bleedin' row with me. Kendell an' me Da are enough at the moment. Christ, the way things are goin', I think someone must be puttin' people up to it."

Each time Joey had the misfortune to meet Kendell on the street, Kendell would leer and promise Joey that he would repay him for "dancin' wit' his girl." Joey would shrug or make some smart comment causing whoever was with him to crack up laughing, making Kendell even more furious.

"Thought you said you had two bits of good news for me?" Joey said, trying to change the subject.

"Yeah," Mick was grinning again. "Trev has arranged a gig for us in the back lounge of The Coach House on Saturday. The manager says that he has to see how good we are before he books us regular. He's payin' us in drink for the first gig."

Joey laughed. "Bloody hell, has anyone told this guy how much we drink? He'll be bleedin' bankrupt!"

Chapter Ten

They agreed to meet in The Coach House at six-thirty to set up their equipment. The gig was to start at eight o'clock and all the lads from school had promised to show up.

"Lads," Ann announced as she arrived in, "I'm shakin'."

"What are you drinking?" the barman asked, looking her up and down in amusement. "Have whatever you want – it'll calm your nerves." He indicated the whole length of the bar as if to confirm his words.

Ann frowned a bit. She looked at all the bottles and then pointing to the Southern Comfort she asked for a double.

"ID?" asked the barman.

Ann made a big deal about looking through her pockets. "Here," she eventually said. "Eighteen last January."

She took the drink from him. "Cheers," she said to the lads. "Here's to us."

Mick laughed. "God, you've expensive taste – not many fellas volunteering to bring you out, I bet."

Ann sneered. "You'd be surprised, Micko. Girls like me don't come cheap but we're quality." She nodded her thanks to the barman and downed the drink in two gulps.

"Wow," Trev said, staring at her. "Even I couldn't do that."

"Medicinal purposes only," Ann replied, grinning. Then, surveying the wires and leads that were all over the floor, she asked if they were nearly ready.

"Almost," Joey was on the ground trying to connect the lights. He looked up at Ann and grinned. "Feck's sake – I hope the audience all have sunglasses with them tonight."

The other three lads tried not to laugh. Trust Joey to say what they had all been thinking. They were afraid Ann might take offence but she just grinned good-naturedly and replied, "Well, there's nothing wrong with trying to light up the room, is there?"

She had excelled herself that evening. Her footwear was the usual purple Doc boots, her jeans were red and she wore an exceptionally bright yellow and red tee-shirt with the words: *The Eight Legged Groove Machine* emblazoned across the front. "Good, huh," she said as she pointed to the slogan.

Joey nodded. "Great album all right," he agreed. It was the title of an album by The Wonderstuff.

"We OK for a sound check?" Trev asked.

Joey nodded as he picked up his guitar. The others took their places as the barman leaned on the bar and listened. When Ann had finished singing the first song he applauded loudly. "Great stuff," he said in admiration as he filled their glasses again. "Go on, drink up, I'm not the one payin' for it," he joked.

The back lounge began to fill up rapidly after that and by seven-thirty there was hardly room to move. A few of the lads from school began a loud chant as they slow clapped: WE WANT LIVEWIRE! WE WANT LIVEWIRE! WHERE THE FECK IS LIVEWIRE?

As they took the floor a huge cheer went up. Joey thought he would die laughing. He and Mick had told the guys to make out that they thought Livewire were brilliant, but this was a bit over the top.

Every song they did, whether it was their own or a cover, received wild applause.

It was when Ann decided to introduce the band to the audience that it descended into the realm of farce. This was not planned and the four lads stopped playing in shock.

"And now," Ann announced. "This cute, blond haired lad with the baby blues, is our very talented drummer – Domo. Stand up Dom and take a bow."

Domo, mortified beyond words, stood up to wolf whistles and cat calls.

"He has a girlfriend, ladies, so you're all out of luck!" Ann said, laughing. Some girl from school pretended to wail with disappointment. Domo glared at Ann's back and sat down.

Ann marched over to Mick next, announcing that he too had a girlfriend and that the relationship was looking very serious. Mick thought it was hilarious and couldn't stop laughing. "I'm open to any offers though," he yelled above the racket. Cathy threw a beer-mat up which hit him across the face, causing more rowdy laughter.

"And this sexy hunk of maleness . . ." Ann began to say as she moved to the front of the stage. Joey got ready to take a bow when he noticed her indicating Trev.

"HEY," Stephen, a guy who lived beside Mick yelled, "BOLAND THOUGHT YOU WERE TALKIN' ABOUT HIM."

Joey went red as the whole place exploded with laughter.

"I bleedin' well did not," he stated vehemently. "Feck off, Steve."

Ann grinned over at him and turning to the audience she asked, "OK, who thinks Joe is a sexy hunk as well?"

There were a lot of noises that sounded vaguely like people being violently sick.

Mick, Trev and Domo were eating themselves laughing. Joey made what he hoped was a sneering type face at his audience and bowed anyway. He began then to pluck a few strings on his guitar, the lead into "Crazy Illusions", a song he had written for the Demo tape. Ann, giving him a huge grin, mercifully began to sing again and some kind of order was restored.

The manager, hearing all the commotion from the main bar, chose this point to enter the proceedings. He liked the song but was even more impressed with the bar takings. He vowed to have Livewire back the next week.

He missed the point where Ann fell off the stage.

She had just launched into a very drunken rendition of The Rembrants "I'll be There for You" when she keeled over. Attempts to lift her failed, she just collapsed in a heap, unable to stop giggling. Then she began to apologise and blamed the barman for plying her with booze. He just shrugged and grinned at her.

The concert had to end early. They were afraid Ann would do herself an injury if she got onstage again. No one minded. Everyone claimed to have had a brilliant time. Joey told them all to ring up the manager in the morning and ask him when that "brilliant" band was coming to play again.

This request was met with cheers and promises of solidarity.

Joey ended up walking Ann home. She kept holding his arm and saying, "Oh, Joe, I'm feeling a bit sick."

Joey tried tactfully to disengage her – he didn't want her puking on his jacket.

"It was good – wasn't it?" Ann asked as she clung onto him.

Joey grinned at her. "Yeah, Ann," he said sincerely. "It was great."

"Don't mind all the others," Ann waved her hand dismissively, "I think you're sexy." She almost fell down then and Joey had to haul her up.

"Get outa tha' garden!" a man, who had been passing by, shouted over.

Joey grinned at him, then turning his attention to his drunken lead singer said, "Thanks, that really does my confidence good after tonight. I needed that."

"Yeah," Ann mumbled, half asleep, "I was afraid they'd hurt your feelings. God, Joe – it was a great night – wasn't it?"

"Yeah," he agreed for the umpteenth time. "It was great."

Chapter Eleven

Joey gazed up at the exam supervisor as she began to give out the English papers. She looked as if she was doing the exam instead of them, he thought. Her face was deathly serious, she didn't even attempt to smile as she said, "OK, turn over your papers now, and good luck to you all."

Joey turned over his page and scanned the essays. The top one was entitled: *My Kind of Music* and he grinned. Picking up his pen he began to write.

Mick had been up since six that morning, swotting. He groaned when he saw the paper. He stuck his pen in his mouth and tried to decide what to tackle first. He decided to read the ultra boring comprehension paragraph and answer the questions on it. He gritted his teeth and began to write a few halting words.

The first exam had begun.

Joey was finished at eleven-thirty. He put down his pen, folded his arms and sprawled himself out in his chair. He gave a deep sigh which caused a few people to look up in irritation. "Sorry," he whispered, causing the exam supervisor to come down the room.

"No talking," she said severely looking down her glasses at him.

"I was only sayin' sorry for sighin' so loud," Joey protested as quietly as he could. "Anyhow, I'm finished. Can I go or wha'?"

She gazed at him with something approaching

disdain. "Have you read through your paper and checked it for spelling mistakes?"

"Yep."

"You may go so."

Joey sauntered up to the top of the room, deposited his paper on the desk and went into the corridor.

There were two fifth years there. They were in charge of bringing in tea and biscuits for the examiner every so often; it was a handy number and the pay was good. Every year there was murder when it came to choosing who would do this job. It was usually those who had done the best over the year.

"Hiya swots!" Joey greeted them cheerily.

They looked up and grinned. "How'd you do, Joe? Was it hard?" asked Mary, a really quiet, shy girl who it seemed was a real Maths whizz kid.

Joey shrugged. "It was all right, I mean how the hell can you fail English, sure you speak it every day for God's sake."

"The afternoon paper's the worst one, isn't it? That's the one with all the poetry in it." Rob, the other fifth year on duty made a face as he said this.

Joey shrugged. "Yeah," he answered, bored with this exam conversation. He didn't want to think beyond lunchtime.

"Do you want some tea and biscuits while you wait for the others to come out?" asked Mary. "We'll join you if you like."

"Great," Joey grinned, never one to turn down anything to eat.

They sat there chatting and laughing quietly till the bell went to say that the first Leaving Cert exam had finished. Students streamed out into the hallway.

Mick came over to him, grinning, "Trust you to

70

flippin' sit here drinkin' tea while the rest of us are sloggin' our brains out in there."

"You could've joined me, couldn't he, Mary?"

She nodded. "You can have some tomorrow," she said in her quiet voice.

"I'll flippin' need more than tea tomorrow," Mick laughed as they began to walk away.

"How'd you do?"

Mick shrugged, "All right, I suppose. I think I passed at least. And you?"

Joey shrugged. "Not bad, well, it wasn't too hard, was it?"

"Glad you thought so," Mick said a bit glumly. "I'm dreading the afternoon though. I hope Wordsworth doesn't come up."

"How'd you do?" Ann caught up with them. "What did you think of the comprehension?"

"All right, it was borin' though," Mick replied. "I did that first."

Joey was glad to get home for lunch the whole discussion over exams bored him.

Dee was in the kitchen, singing loudly in accompaniment to the radio.

"Ouch," Joey, grinning, put his hands to his ears.

She whirled around, blushing at being caught. "Shut up you," she laughed. "I got a pay rise today."

"Yeah? Great stuff." Joey grinned as he flung his jacket on a chair.

"How'd you get on?" Dee asked.

"All right, I guess. Things went my way though."

"They'd want to, after the little bit of study you did. Trust you!"

Joey laughed as he went to put on the kettle.

Dee settled back into the kitchen chair saying, "Give your eldest sister a treat and make the lunch."

"Janey, it's you that should be makin' it for me," Joey said as he got a few eggs from the fridge. "I'm worn out after that exam."

Dee giggled. "That'll be the day." She watched her brother cracking the eggs to make a couple of omelettes. He cursed as half a shell fell in to the pan.

"Joe," she ventured hesitantly.

"Mmm."

"When are you going to talk to Da?"

"Aw, Dee," he groaned. "Not again."

"When, Joe?" she persisted.

"Just forget it," he grinned. "Relax."

"How can I relax?" Dee exclaimed. "The tension in this house is awful. Da's really sorry he hit you, you know he is."

"Look," Joey began, "if I don't talk, how can we fight?" This was said with such charm that Dee, despite herself smiled hopelessly. "That's stupid, Joe. You know it is."

Joey's easy smile vanished and he said seriously, "I'm goin' to do what I want. I am goin' to play music an' if he doesn't like it, well, tough shit!"

"He thinks that there's no future in music."

"No disrespect, Dee, but where the hell is the future in medicine or the future in being a lawyer or a train driver or bleedin' anythin' – no jobs about that I can see."

He was getting upset, Dee could tell. She decided that there was no point in saying any more. She didn't want to put him off his exam that afternoon. "Touché," she grinned and then, "Oh – Joey – the eggs are burning – quick, grab the pan!"

They had toast for their lunch. Joey ate all the bread bar the heel – he decided to leave that as Chris would have a fit if there was no bread left when she came home.

Joey arrived home late that evening. He had been over at Mick's helping him with his Maths for the next day.

"How did you get on?" Chris demanded, the minute she saw him.

"Fine."

"What do you mean, 'fine'?" Chris asked. "Is that good or what?"

"It's fine, that's all!" Joey grinned.

"Well, if that's the extent of your vocabulary, I don't fancy your chances of passing," Mr Boland said gruffly.

Joey's grin vanished, but other than that he showed no reaction to the fact that his Da had spoken. "What culinary delights have you concocted for me dinner?" he asked Chris as he began to set a place for himself at the table.

"I'd a good mind not to cook you anything, seeing as all the bread was gone when I came home," Chris said accusingly.

"Why, what were you goin' to make, bread pudding or somethin'?"

Chris giggled. "Smart ass – just don't eat all the bread on me again – right!"

"I didn't mean to, it's just that we burnt the lunch."

"*We* – I like that," Dee yelled. "You burnt the lunch, baby bruv, not me!"

Mr Boland heaved himself off the chair stating, "There is not a lot you can do, is there, Joe?"

Joey made a face behind his back and began to apply himself with vigour to his dinner. Nodding to where his Da had gone out he said, "Is it me or is he in shit form?"

"It's you," both his sisters said in unison.

Chapter Twelve

The week after the Leaving Cert ended Livewire turned up at the National Concert Hall on Dublin's southside to enter the second round of Battle of the Bands.

"You guys must be Livewire." It was a statement rather than a question. The five nodded. "Follow me so," said the weirdest looking lady they had ever seen – pink hair, pink make-up, pink clothes. Even Ann paled by comparison.

"Guess you must like pink, huh?" Mick had it said before he realised it. To his surprise the woman laughed. She turned to him and said jokingly, "Can't feckin' stand it!" The others grinned, even Ann, who was pale with nerves.

She led them onto a large stage and waved her arm around as she said, "OK, folks, it's all yours. Take your time, we'll be on the other side of the curtain." She gave them a demonstration on how to pull the curtain.

There was a stunned silence when she left. "For feck's sake," Trev sounded annoyed as he whirled on Mick. "She is one of the judges an' you have to comment on her dress sense. Great bleedin' start."

Mick shrugged helplessly. "How was I supposed to know?" He was busy examining the keyboard that they had provided. It was a bit like his own one. Trev would not let the subject drop. He continued to moan at Mick until Joey told him to "shut the hell up".

Trev glared at Joe then and was about to give an acidic retort when he was stopped in his tracks by one of the judges asking, "Are you ready?"

"Just a sec," Ann yelled, glad of the distraction. She turned to the two of them and hissed, "Will you both cop on and get your acts together. Do you want to enter this thing or what?"

Both lads turned to their guitars and began to tune up. Joey gave her a quick grin and a half salute. He thought Ann was hilarious when she bossed Trev about. Trev would never answer her back.

When they were ready Ann pulled the curtain back to reveal three judges – two men and the Pink Lady.

"Now lads," said the older man as he placed his arms on the table in front of him and leaned in toward the stage, "any song from your demo tape will do. I trust you have one picked out?"

"Yeah – it's called 'Crazy Illusions'," Trev replied.

The manager of The Coach House loved this song and insisted that they play it at all of their gigs

They began to play. The colour came back to Ann's face as she started to sing. The judges had been writing until they heard her voice. Their heads shot up as they studied her intensely. When the song ended, the Pink Lady smiled saying, "You will know in a couple of months what the story is. The finals are in late October and will be televised. Three original songs are needed, so you should get working on them just in case."

"How many will qualify?" Mick asked.

"Eight."

"How many bands are you hearin'?" Mick asked, interested. Trev was poking him in the back, wanting to shut him up. This made him more determined than ever to ask.

"'bout five hundred."

The five onstage gasped and she laughed at their shocked faces as she said, "There are a lot of bands out there, you know!"

They left the hall feeling quite dejected.

"Five hundred bands," wailed Ann. "Janey, we haven't a hope."

"That's nice," Joey pretended to be insulted. "I wrote the song an' you sang it, you've obviously got great faith in our combined talents."

"I didn't mean it like that," Ann protested.

"I agree with Ann," Domo said quietly. "It is a long shot."

"Not when you're as good as we are," Trev tried to sound confident. His own heart had sunk – why the hell did Mick have to ask?

"I saw the oul fella look up when Joe did his guitar solo," Mick declared.

"Yeah?" Joey was interested.

"Yeah."

"Did he look impressed, you know, as if he liked it?"

"Eh – yeah."

"What way did he look?" Joey pressed eagerly.

"Eh –'bout fortyish, grey suit, didn't get the colour of his eyes . . ."

"Ha, ha."

Joey pounced on Mick and the two began to wrestle, slagging each other and laughing. Ann and Domo grinned. Trev told them scornfully to "grow up". They ignored him and walked on ahead. When they reached the top of Grafton Street they waited for the others to catch up.

"We're goin' into McDonald's for a burger," Mick said. "Anyone else comin' along?"

Ann and Domo readily agreed.

Trev said that he had to go to Merrion Square and collect some soccer tickets.

The four went into McDonald's and stuffed themselves with Big Macs. They spent about an hour analysing their performance and decided that they had done the best they could.

It was time to go at last. Mick kept looking at his watch and eventually said, "Look lads, I have to go. I have to do a bit of shopping, you know."

Joey stared at him. "Wha'? You hate shoppin'. Are you buying something special?"

"Naw!" Mick was too off-hand. Joey knew he was hiding something. "Well, what is it then? What is the big shoppin' spree for?"

"I never said it was a shoppin' spree," Mick protested weakly, inwardly cursing Joey.

"So, what are you gettin'?"

"None of your bleedin' business," Mick snapped.

"Ouch," Joey grinned.

"It's a birthday present for Cath, if you must know."

"Oh, that's great, Mick. What are you buying her?" Ann was impressed.

He shrugged. "Dunno, haven't got a clue. I think jewellery or somethin'."

Ann offered to go with him and help him decide. He looked at her doubtfully and said as tactfully as he could, "Normal kinda jewellery, Ann."

She laughed and nodded. "Yeah, I know, come on, let's get going," She dragged him off his chair and turning to the others asked if they wanted to come as well.

"Aw, here," Mick protested, taken aback.

"Let's go," Joey rubbed his hands and winked at Ann. "Now, where to first?"

Domo and he pretended not to hear Mick's carefully chosen expletives as they pushed him out onto the street.

Chapter Thirteen

A dull humid August morning dawned. Joey's alarm
clock went off at nine. He groaned and, without
opening his eyes, he began to feel along the desk by
his bedside. His fingers marched the length and
breath of it, knocking over tapes, CDs and issues of
Hot Press which fell to the floor with dull thuds,
adding to the noise of the loud bell. Joey pulled a
pillow over his head in a feeble attempt to blot out
the sound of the loud ringing but it was no use.

The bloody alarm clock was over beside the door
– he would have to get out of bed to switch it off. He
had done this last night to force himself to get out of
bed to do some songwriting. Trev went mad
yesterday when Joey had again declared that he had
been unable to write anything. "Me muse has
deserted me," he had said jokingly. This had been
received by four blank stares. None of them had been
amused. Domo had even made some kind of smart
comment. Ann, who normally laughed at Joey's
excuses, had sided with Trev. Mick had offered to
help him but Joey had firmly and politely refused. He
wrote his songs alone – fair enough if the others
wanted to change them after they had been written,
he didn't mind, but they were *his* songs.

He switched off the alarm, threw on an old pair of

jeans and a tee-shirt, went into the kitchen, grabbed a bowl of flakes for breakfast and carried them back upstairs to his room. He opened a drawer in his desk and pulled out a sheaf of papers – tunes that he had written at various stages. There were lyrics also. Joey carefully discarded each one until he came to some barely legible notes on a dirty, dog-eared piece of paper. He scanned the page and his eyes shone – it was perfect! No other band would have anything like it – if they got through of course. He even remembered writing the tune. It was when they had been studying *Kubla Khan* in English Class. It was the only poem that had truly captured Joey's imagination. During class, while the teacher was analysing the poem, he had jotted down some notes. He had always meant to finish it but obviously he had forgotten to do so.

The English book was buried somewhere in his wardrobe, carelessly thrown in when his exams had finished. He felt fairly confident that he remembered the words of the poem, but he decided to be on the safe side so, rummaging through the chaos that was his wardrobe he eventually found it. He flicked to the page and began to jot down notes beside it. He could hear the sound of the music in his head, the sound of the drums signalling the war to come, the building in progress. The guitar solo, high chords and low chords showing the battle – a bit like De Burgh's "Crusaders", the lighter notes at the end. He chopped and changed the poem to suit his music, making sure it never lost its shape and power.

It took him four hours to complete the job and he was well satisfied with the result. He couldn't wait to go to rehearsal the next day and show it to the others.

His mind was buzzing with music now and tunes floated in and out of it. It didn't take him long to think of another idea. He had all his work completed by four in the afternoon. His stomach growled and he remembered with some surprise that he had not had any lunch. He decided to wander downstairs and see what he could find in the press. He found a packet of crisps and, pouring himself some juice, he carried his grub into the den. Chris was sitting watching some stupid film on the television. She had a box of tissues beside her. Joey offered her a crisp and she nearly took the whole packet from him. "Hungry, are you?" he joked.

Chris nodded, grinning at him. Then, looking with disgust at his clothes she remarked, "You'd better change into something a bit newer for dinner today."

"Why?"

"Irene is coming and Da wants us all there."

Joey made no comment. He had hoped that Irene would exit from their lives, but it was not happening. He wondered if there was a way he could avoid having dinner with his family. He could have gone to Mick's for some grub, but Mick was going out this afternoon. There was no way he could afford to go to the chipper and he was not depriving himself of his dinner just to make a point. The best way, he decided, would be to sit through it and ignore his oul fella and his "lady friend". There was no way he was going ta bleedin' dress up for them either – they could just take him as he was.

At six o'clock, the Boland family, plus Irene, sat down to what promised to be a delicious meal.

"Joe," Dee yelled, "dinner!"

They all looked up in horror as he arrived in the back door. He was filthy! His jeans were covered in muck, his shirt was ruined, his face and hands were manky.

"Doin' a bit of gardenin', don't suppose I've time to change?" he asked, knowing perfectly well that he hadn't.

"Since when have you been into gardening?" Dee asked, disbelief and disgust written all over her face.

"Since this afternoon." He gazed insolently at his treacherous sisters.

Chris gave him a filthy look, which he ignored.

"Go and wash your hands," his father growled.

Joey slowly began wiping his hands on his jeans, giving them all the full benefit of his appearance. He left the kitchen.

Mr Boland turned to Irene saying, "Try and ignore him. It's all done to get at me."

Irene had brought a bottle of wine and all had a glass except Joey, who had refused with a curt, "No."

There was an uncomfortable silence but Chris eased it over by saying, "I'm glad to see you've given up the booze, Joe." She gave him no chance to reply but kept prattling on.

He ate in silence, not partaking in any of the jokes and stories that were exchanged. He caught his Da looking oddly at him and he returned the stare with as much brazenness as he could muster.

It was after the tea that the bombshell was dropped.

Joey watched with horror his as Da put his arm round Irene and give her shoulder the slightest of squeezes. She gave a nervous smile, glanced uneasily at Joey and shook her head slightly. His Da squeezed her shoulder again and stood up.

"I wanted the three of you here today to tell you something."

Chris and Dee looked up with interest. Joey felt sick. He thought he knew what was coming.

"Irene and I are going to get engaged." Mr Boland blushed and smiled at his future bride. She took his hand and looked round at the three of them.

"I know it must come as a bit of a shock to you all," she said gently. "But we love each other and want to be together. I know you will want your Dad to be happy."

"Of course we do." Chris jumped up and flung her arms around her father. "I'm so happy for you, Da. I'm so glad you can be happy again." She included Irene in her hug then.

Dee smiled at them. "I'm glad he got someone like you, Irene. You're a lot like Ma."

"No way!" Joey made them all jump. "How can you say that? She is not like our Ma and she'll never replace her either!" He glared at Irene as he hissed, "You can't ever replace her, you know!" He turned to his sisters. Anger and hurt shone in his eyes. His voice was trembling. "How can you be so happy? It's not right. What about Ma? What about her – huh?" This last part was directed at his father. His voice faltered as he asked, "How can you forget her? She was our Ma!" He stared at them for what seemed like ages.

His Da was staring at the table, his arm defensively around Irene who had gone pale and seemed about to cry. Dee and Chris looked shocked at the outburst.

Joey picked up a wine glass. He held it up in a mock toast. "Have a nice bleedin' evenin'," he said sneeringly. He turned on his heel and left the house, slamming the door as loudly as he could.

He vomited into the rosebush.

Chapter Fourteen

The last two weeks had been bleedin' hell. Dee and
Chris were barely talking to him. His Da and Irene
had had a terrible row; when he had arrived back that
awful night they had been yelling at each other. Irene
had been saying that he shouldn't have broken the
news to them in that manner and his Da yelling back
that no matter what way the news had been broken
that his, Joe's reaction would have been the same – at
least he agreed with his Da on that one.

He had told Mick over lunch.

"Me Da is gettin' married again." There, he had
said it!

Mick gulped. He looked at his best mate. What
was he supposed to say? "To yer one – Irene?"

Joe nodded miserably.

"I'm sorry for you, Joe. I know how you feel. Your
Da has to live his life an' all but I'd still hate it if my
Da married someone else."

Joey shrugged. "Thanks for sayin' that, Mick."

"No problem."

There was more hell to come. The Leaving Cert
results were out. He had to call to Mick on the way
to the school. Dee met him going out the door. She
gave him a tentative smile saying, "Good luck, Joe."

83

He grinned at her, glad at least that one person in the house was speaking to him. "You'll be the first to know the news, sis."

Mick was waiting impatiently for him to arrive. He was a nervous wreck and Joey felt guilty that he didn't feel a bit more anxious. In order not to get on Mick's nerves he pretended to be worried.

When they arrived at their school, students were milling around all over the place – there were tears and screams of delight as they opened the small brown envelopes.

Mick and Joey made their way to the secretary's office. There was a queue but it was moving rapidly. Finally, Mick's turn came. The secretary handed him his envelope saying, "I hope it's what you want." He thanked her and fled.

Joey was gazing after Mick to see where he had gone. "Name?" barked the secretary.

"Joseph Boland," he told her.

She searched through the envelopes and found his results. As she handed them to him she said, "Rumour has it you did quite well."

Joey didn't know if she was being sarcastic or not. He grinned at her, stuffed the envelope in his pocket and went to find Mick.

He found him leaning up against the gym wall trying to do mental calculations. "I think I'm ten bleedin' points short, Joe!" he groaned. "That's going on last year's point requirements. Flippin' great!"

Joey took Mick's results from him and added it himself. "You've three hundred and fifty points," he announced.

Mick nodded. "That's what I thought. Ten points short."

"You'll get in on the second round," Joey replied confidently. "Dee was loads of points short for her course an' she got in on the third round – relax about it."

"That's bleedin' easy for you to say – you couldn't give a damn about it."

"So-rry," Joey drawled, hand in the air. "I was only tryin' to cheer you up."

Mick nodded. "Yeah, I know." Then, "How did you do, anyhow?"

They were walking toward the school gates.

"Dunno." Joey searched in his pockets for the envelope as Mick suppressed a grin. Trust Joe!

Joey tore open his results, read them and stuffed them back into his jacket. "OK," he replied.

"Well, do I not get a look?" asked Mick puzzled.

"Ah, what for? Sure, what good is it to you?"

Joey was being evasive.

"You didn't fail, did you?" Mick sounded worried and incredulous.

Joey grinned. "Aw, no. I did fine."

"Huh – I bleedin' show you my results an' you don't flippin' bother to return the favour. I'd never have thought you were like that Joe."

Joey sighed. He had hoped Mick would let it pass, but clearly not. "Here!" He shoved his results into his mate's hand.

Mick opened up the scrunched-up paper and his eyes widened. "Bloody hell, Joe."

Joe shrugged.

"They're flipping great. Four A1s, two A2s and a B1. Jaysus, what the hell would you have got if you had studied!"

"Dunno."

"You could do anythin' on those results."

85

Mick was gazing at him in awe.

"Yeah, well, I am not goin' to college. I am flippin' sick of bleedin' school. Just forget about it, Mick." He took the results from him and said, "I feel rotten, me gettin' the kinda results you need."

Mick laughed. "For feck's sake, don't be a bleedin' moron. I wouldn't have even passed Maths if it wasn't for you bein' so brainy. Janey, it makes a change from the Mock – huh?"

"Are you goin' out tonight to celebrate?" Joey changed the subject.

Mick grinned. "Yeah, 'course. Everyone is meetin' at the school. We'll decide where we are goin' then. I dunno if Cath will be going. I think her crew are all going out somewhere as well. Anyhow, call for me – right!"

"Sure."

Mick left him and walked into his house and Joey continued walking home.

He arrived home at three o'clock. He had called into a few friends' houses and ended up staying for a while.

Dee flung open the door as he arrived in the driveway. Chris was at her heels.

"Were you afraid to come home?" she asked anxiously.

"We thought that you had done somethin' stupid." Chris was nearly in tears.

Joey felt guilty. He had stayed out deliberately, as he knew they would be dying to know. He wanted them to sweat in order to punish them for ignoring him the past two weeks.

"Naw, I'm grand," he declared, walking into the kitchen. His Da was there already. He must have come home early today.

Mr Boland breathed an invisible sigh of relief as he saw his son. He had honestly been terrified that Joe had gone off the rails – maybe that easy exterior had been a front?

"Well, how did you do?" Dee demanded.

Mr Boland tried to look disinterested.

Joey pulled his results from his pocket and handed them to his eldest sister. She squealed when she read them. She flung her arms around her brother and proceeded to dance around the kitchen with him yelling, "Well done, Joe. Brilliant stuff!"

Chris had to sit down in shock. She kept saying, "How did you do it, Joe?"

"Am I to be kept in suspense?" Mr Boland's voice cut through the festivities. Joey stopped grinning as Dee handed her father the results. There was silence in the kitchen.

Mr Boland couldn't believe his eyes. How the hell had Joe managed it? He hadn't done a bloody tap!

"He did great, didn't he, Da?" Dee gulped, breaking the silence.

"Eh – yeah," Mr Boland stammered. He looked up at his son, who as usual had that sulky countenance, hands stuck deep into pockets, eyes narrowed. "Well done, Joe," he said sincerely. "I'm glad to see that you came to your senses. You will be able to do anything on those results."

Joey bristled. He bit his lip and said, "Yeah, Da. I'm goin' to write music."

Dee thought her father would go through the roof! "He gets a brilliant Leaving," he roared, glaring at his two daughters, "and he just throws it away."

Then he gulped and his voice dropped as he sat

down. "Oh, sweet Jesus," he groaned. "Will you get real, Joe?"

Joey advanced on him. He spoke quietly. "Naw Da, you get real. I want to play music, I want to write music. It's my bleedin' life and you can't live it for me."

"You'll have no security for the future – that's the reason I want you to do something. But you are too stupid and too lazy to recognise that! YOU ARE A WASTER! A WASTER! All you can do is write stupid songs that no one will ever listen to! We all know what kind of fellas go into the music business – don't we?"

"Dad!" Chris exclaimed, shocked.

Joey gave his Dad a despairing look. "Thanks, Da. Thanks a lot!"

With these words he picked up his Leaving Cert results, tore it in half and half again saying, "That's how much it means to me." He left the kitchen.

Dee gazed at her father and whispered, "That was a bit below the belt, Da. It was a bit mean."

"That kid is my flippin' cross in life," he said savagely. "What the hell did I do to deserve him?"

Chapter Fifteen

They were going to Club Sarah. Cathy had decided to accompany Mick after all. Trev and Domo went as well "for the crack". Trev drove Joey, Mick, Cathy and Domo up. Ann had said that she would make her own way and see them there.

It took thirty minutes for the car to arrive. It looked like the whole of sixth year was queuing outside. Ann spotted Mick and came over. "Hi," she smiled. "How'd you do?" There was more exam talk which bored Joey until Ann gave him a dig in the ribs saying, "I heard you did brilliant, you swot."

He shrugged. "I had my reasons."

He smiled at her and she lightly touched his arm as she said softly, "Well done." They had become great friends since that day in the park.

"You and your mates sitting with us?" Cathy asked Ann. "I don't know anyone here and it would be brilliant to have someone I know sitting at our table."

"Sure," Ann exclaimed. "I'll just get the others."

The disco was jam packed. They were lucky to find a table at all. They had to rob seats. There were ten people sitting at the table and Cathy was glad that she had asked Ann to join them as Ann kept her involved in the conversation and introduced her to everyone – something Mick would never think of doing.

Everyone was up dancing except Ann and Joey.

"What did your Da think of the results?" she asked.

Joey took a gulp of his pint. He stared into his glass as he told her the story. "It didn't go according to plan," he said with a grin.

Ann sighed. "Ah, well, at least you did OK. He can't give out about that." She grabbed his arm saying, "Come on and let's join the others."

At ten o'clock, the DJ slowed it down. Everyone began to make their way off the dance floor.

Before Ann reached the edge of the floor, she felt a hand on her shoulder.

"Dancin'?" a harsh voice asked.

Ann turned around. She was facing a tall, unshaven, denim clad youth. He had earrings up both ear-lobes and a stud in his nose. He looked filthy.

"No thanks." She said it as politely as she could.

She turned to leave, but the grip tightened on her shoulder. "Why the bleedin' hell not?"

"Because my boyfriend wouldn't like it," she replied, as calmly as possible, glibly telling the trusted lie all girls use now and again for getting rid of undesirables.

"Oh, yeah," the lad mocked, breathing alcohol fumes into her face, "and where the hell is he, then?" He pulled her roughly to him, hissing in her ear, "Come on, one dance won't kill you!"

"Get your hands off me," Ann pushed against him. She felt a bit frightened. "I'm not dancing with you."

"Well, I want to dance with you. Let's see who wins!" He pulled her even closer.

"Get your paws off her, Kendell!"

Ann, with relief, recognised Joey's voice.

90

Kendell looked up. "Joe bloody Boland," he spat. "The self-appointed bleedin' knight in shinin' armour for helpless women. You gonna make me leave her alone?"

Joey took his arm and hissed, "Don't tempt me!"

"Jaysus, is this your boyfriend?" He asked Ann, and then without waiting for a reply, he said viciously, "I wouldn't trust him." He shoved Ann at Joey who caught her and kept his arm around her as she was shaking slightly.

"I'm warnin' you Boland – I'll get you! I'll bleedin' get you! As for that bitch – " he pointed at Ann, "The only reason I asked you to dance is because you look like some kinda multi-coloured weirdo. I thought you'd be game for anything."

Joey caught Kendell before he had a chance to walk away. He dug his fingers into his shoulder blades, causing him to wince. "You are a bleedin' asshole, Kendell. You shut your mouth." He shook him, leered into his face and hissed, "I bleedin' swear if you come near her again, I'll finish you." He pushed Kendell, grabbed Ann and with his arm around her he walked her into the hall where it was quiet. Behind him he could hear Kendell still issuing threats.

He sat Ann down on a chair and asked awkwardly, "Are you OK?" He pretended not to see her hastily wiping away a tear that had strayed down her cheek. He felt angry that someone should dare to treat her in this way – she was too bleedin' nice.

She nodded, averting her face. "I'm fine, thanks."

Joey didn't know what to say to her; he was useless in these situations. He sought vainly for a female he knew, surely they would know what to do. He was out of luck.

He swallowed and said gently, "Don't mind what he said, Ann. The guy is a headcase. He's high on dope half the time, when he's not drinkin' that is. He's been inside for joy-riding. I'm tellin' you, he's a bleedin' nutter."

Then nodding, he finished up, "He's a feckin' eejit. I'm only sorry I didn't see him comin' over to you sooner."

There was a silence and then Joey said, "Are you ready to come inside? I promise, the next set of slows – I'm all yours!"

Ann laughed. "God, there's not much choice, either you or Kendell." She pretended to consider and then said, "I think I'll take my chances with him!"

"Bleedin' gratitude!"

At the next set of slows, as good as his word, Joey asked Ann up to dance. There was a lot of good-natured slagging at this, but they both laughed it off. He took her into the middle of the dance floor saying, "He won't be able to spot you in this crowd."

"Thanks Joe," Ann said as she placed her hands loosely on his shoulders.

"Forget it."

They started to talk about other things and he had her laughing at his exploits with Mick the summer before last. They had decided to work for the summer, doing odd jobs for people.

"Oh stop, Joe," Ann giggled. "I don't know whether you are making those stories up or what, but just don't tell me anymore, I've a pain from laughing."

"One more?" Joey enjoyed making her laugh. She had the most attractive smile, he thought.

Ann wasn't listening. She had spotted Kendell

through the crowd and had caught her breath. "Oh Joe," she tried to make her voice sound normal. "I think he's coming back this way."

Joey turned and gave Kendell a wave. "That'll feckin' drive him nuts," he joked. He looked at Ann then. She wasn't laughing. "Are you all right?"

Ann shook her head. "He's going to stare at us all night, Joe. I think I'd prefer to go home. I just know he's going to ruin my night and I don't want to give him the satisfaction."

Joey laughed. "He's not goin' to cause any hassle Ann – he's all mouth, honest."

But try as he might, Joey couldn't persuade her to stay. He offered to go home with her but she refused.

"Just go and see if there is a taxi outside while I get my coat," Ann said as she went in the direction of the cloakroom. "I'll wait for you there."

Joey shrugged and did as he was told.

It was while Ann was getting her coat that she noticed Kendell and a few others standing at the entrance to the disco. She turned her face to the wall so that they wouldn't notice her. A minute or so later she worked up the courage to turn around again. The group had gone. Ann breathed a sigh of relief.

She began to get worried when Joey didn't arrive back. He had been gone ten minutes and taxis weren't that hard to find – there was always the odd one waiting outside.

She waited for another couple of minutes, her stomach churning with nerves. Still no sign of Joey.

Ann marched back into the dance area and tried desperately to locate a sign of Kendell. She would have given anything for him to march up to her and drag her onto the dance floor. She couldn't see him.

Her heart began to hammer and suddenly – in one sickening moment – Ann knew what had happened. She looked around the room frantically.

She knew she had to find Mick or one of the lads from school. She began to panic – Joey had been gone over fifteen minutes.

Mick was startled when she appeared at his side, looking pale. "Are you OK?" he asked anxiously. "I thought Joe was with you. Is Kendell bothering you?"

Ann shook her head and said breathlessly, "Mick, Joe went to get me a taxi about fifteen minutes ago. He hasn't come back – Kendell is gone too – I can't see him anywhere. I just know they're going after him, Mick. I just know it." Her voice broke.

"You sure?" Mick asked, gripping her by the shoulders as Ann nodded.

"Shit!" Mick went white. "Kendell is dangerous. Joe is always laughing him off."

"Oh, Mick," Ann said anxiously. "What are we going to do?"

He turned to Cathy and said, "Round up as many lads as you can find. Tell them to meet me at the entrance in five minutes."

Within moments, there were fifteen lads waiting for Mick to arrive.

"We're coming along as well," Cathy announced, pulling on her coat. Her tone broached no argument as Mick well knew.

"You had better look after yerselves so," he replied narkily. "I don't have time to be molly-coddling you."

"Feck off, Mick," Cathy was irritated. "You remind me of Julian from the *Famous Five*."

94

There was a guffaw of laughter and Mick gave her a filthy look. Ann, despite being worried sick, managed a smile.

Outside, the air was cool, the night calm. There was only one place that Kendell and his mates could have brought Joey without attracting attention and with Mick leading they all began to jog in that direction.

Once he got outside, Joey began to walk briskly. He couldn't believe that Ann would let her night be ruined by that no-hoper. He walked around the side of the disco where the taxis were usually parked . . .

Before he knew what was happening, Joey was grabbed from behind.

His hair was pulled back as a blindfold was tightened around his head. He could feel his hands being pulled together behind his back.

"Wha –" he managed to say before he was silenced by a slam across his face. This was followed by two more, causing his head to spin. A cloth of some sort was stuffed into his mouth.

"You shut up," a voice from the darkness, a voice he was too dazed to recognise. "You just shut up," the voice repeated in a eerie, silent way.

Joey felt himself being half dragged, half pulled somewhere. He stumbled a few times and was kicked when he fell down. His heart began to hammer fiercely. The sound drummed in his ears, making him think he would faint. It seemed they walked for ages, but in effect it was only five minutes. Eventually, he was let go and the silence of the night pressed in on Joey.

"You are goin' to be taught a lesson, one I don't think you'll forget." The voice again.

There was a metallic click and the cold edge of a penknife was laid against his face. Joey gulped – beads of sweat broke out on his brow.

"Aw, here, I don't think –" a voice from behind.

"YOU SHUT UP," the other voice hissed. "WHAT'S THE MATTER – YOU CHICKEN?"

"I thought we were only goin' to give him a bashing."

"So we are – a real good bashin' and then when he conks out, I'll carve his face up real good." The voice sounded caressing. Once again the penknife was laid against Joey's face. He could feel it cutting into him and the trickle of blood that followed.

"That's only for starters!" There was the sound of lunatic laughter and then a terrible punch was landed square on his face.

Joey could feel the burst of blood from his nose. He thought he was going to choke; it was getting harder and harder to breathe. He tried to spit the gag from his mouth.

He began to struggle against the hands that were holding him.

He fell to his knees, hurting them badly. When he was kicked in the stomach, he gasped.

"Shut your face, asshole."

He was kicked again and again and again. He tried to roll away but they wouldn't stop.

He couldn't even struggle now. He was growing immune to the pain. There was a welcoming blackness . . .

"STOP THEM!" The shout reverbrated down the laneway. Eighteen bodies hurled themselves toward the six lads that were standing around a motionless figure.

The six began to run.

Cathy and Ann had been told to stay where they were. Ann began to walk toward the lane. "Come on, Cath. I'm not staying here. Let's see if Joe is OK. We got here in good time, he can't be too bad."

Together they approached the laneway. They saw Mick and a few of the other lads kneeling down on the ground. As they got closer, they noticed with horror a body splayed in a grotesque position on the cement path.

Mick, pale and shocked, gazed at them both. "Steve is gone to telephone an ambulance," he whispered.

"What!" Cathy screamed in shock. "Is he all right – is he, Mick?"

Mick was white. She thought he was going to collapse. "We can't wake him, Cath. We can't wake him."

Ann had begun to scream.

Mick reached for Cathy's hand. She hugged him saying, "Come on, Mick. Please don't cry."

Mick's voice broke. He held her fiercely. "He's me best mate, Cath. If anything happens to him –"

97

Chapter Sixteen

Casualty was crazy tonight. Irene had been called down from ward duty to help bridge the gap. She passed a hand across her forehead and tried to fight the tiredness.

She braced herself to receive the next ambulance. They had radioed ahead to say that they had picked up a badly beaten youth. They had given him a blood transfusion but he was totally unconscious. Irene hated this job sometimes, especially when a young person was involved.

The ambulance screeched to a halt. The stretcher was removed and the ambulance men began to run toward her with it. As she looked at the body on the stretcher, her first thought was that there was so much blood. There was blood on the lad's hair, face, hands and clothes. When she looked a bit closer, she froze.

"What is his name?" she asked the ambulance man faintly.

"Joe, his name is Joe Boland," replied the girl who had accompanied the stretcher.

Irene turned to the girl. There was a lad with her.

"Does his father know?" Irene asked Mick hastily, and then added, "I know his Dad."

Mick numbly shook his head. "Cops said they'd tell him."

"Look," Irene said, indicating two chairs, "Wait here. I'll be back as soon as I can, OK?"

Mick helped Ann into the chair. She hadn't said a word since she had screamed in the laneway. She had clung dumbly to Joe's hand all the way to the hospital.

Irene beckoned to another nurse and asked to be relieved. She then ran to the phone in her office. She dialled Pete's number, vainly wondering what she was going to say to him.

"Hello?" A sleepy voice that she recognised as Pete's answered the phone.

"Hi, Pete, it's me."

"Irene," he exclaimed. "Are you OK? Is there something wrong?"

"It's Joe —"

Pete laughed. "You call me at two in the morning cause you're worried about Joe! Irene, I keep telling you, he's only a kid. Don't let him ruin everything."

"He's here, Pete." Irene couldn't find the words to tell him. She hoped he would get the message that something was wrong. She wished she hadn't rung, but she didn't want the cops frightening the hell out of him.

"There?" Pete was still sleepy. "What on earth is he doing at your place?"

"I'm still at work, Pete. He's — he's here, at the hospital." She gulped as she continued, "He's been brought in. He's —"

"Is he OK?" Pete suddenly understood.

"He's in a bad way." Irene could feel the tears coming. "Pete, you'd better come right away."

At three in the morning, Irene entered the small casualty waiting room. She was taken aback to see about twenty people jump up when she asked to see the ones that had come in with Joe Boland. The policeman who had been put on the case had finished taking their statements and was just leaving.

"Any news?" Cathy asked.

Irene gazed around at them all and was touched at their concern for Joey. "Sorry to have kept you all so long," she apologised. "I think the best thing you can all do at this point is to go home and get some sleep. There is nothing you can do here tonight. You won't be allowed to see him – I'm sorry."

"How is he?"

Irene bit her lip. They were all only kids, how did you tell them that their friend was in a bad way?

"I'm not leavin' here till I bleedin' know how he is!" Mick had advanced toward her. He was totally dishevelled. "How can I bleedin' go home and Joe in here? You tell me that – huh?"

"Mick!" Cathy put her hand on his arm. "You heard her, we can do nothing here." She gazed at Irene. "Is there no news?"

Irene took a deep breath. "He's in the Intensive Care Unit," she began. "To be frank with all of you, he's not in good shape. He has lost a lot of blood and he is pretty badly beaten up. That's all I know for now."

There was a horrible silence.

Ann began to moan and Trev put his arm around her. He felt sickened.

Mick dropped into the nearest chair and put his head in his hands. He honestly thought he would puke. He knew if he stood up he would probably fall right back down again. Cathy put her arms around him and rested her head on his head, saying nothing.

Perhaps it was this gesture that made Irene say, "Well, if you want, you can stay here. It won't be very comfortable. You can use the telephone in my office to ring your folks." She looked at them all questioningly.

"Fine and thanks," Stephen, who had phoned the ambulance, spoke for them all.

"Will you let us know if there is any change?" another lad said.

Irene nodded. "Sure I will."

Irene walked into the IC Unit and kissed the top of Pete Boland's head.

"Where are Chris and Dee?" he asked.

"I sent them home," Irene said. "I gave them a list of stuff to get for Joe and they are bringing it in tomorrow. Chris is too emotional to stay here tonight. Dee is looking after her."

Mr Boland nodded. He ran his finger gently down the side of his son's face. "How could anyone do this to him, Irene?" His voice broke into a sob. "Look at his face – they used a penknife on this part, that's what the doctor said."

"When the stitches heal, it won't be so noticable," she consoled him.

"They broke his nose and . . . and . . . his . . . leg. They stamped on his leg, Irene. They smashed his nose! They tried to kill –" Pete's voice was rising in hysteria.

Irene held him. "I know, Pete. I know."

When he had calmed down she asked if he wanted

her to stay with him. He shook his head saying, "Thanks, Irene, but I just want to be by myself."

"I'll see you first thing in the morning so," she said gently as she left.

Pete Boland began the longest night of his life. A prayer of sorts began a slow tattoo inside his brain. "Please, God, don't let him die. Please, God, don't let him die." Over and over again it went as all the rows he and his son had had paraded themselves before him. He willed himself to stop thinking of these things but he couldn't. He and Joe had barely talked these last few months and now it might be too late.

There was complete silence inside the IC Unit, the only light coming from all the monitors his son was hooked up to. Joey's face was lit by a greenish glow, making him look worse than ever. His face was pale underneath the bruises and the tan he picked up by "just looking at the sun" as Dee so enviously put it.

Mr Boland gently stroked Joe's hair. His gaze wandered to Joe's eyes, which looked almost girlish with their long, curly lashes.

"Please, son, don't leave me," he silently begged.

He remembered Joey being born and how thrilled he and Marie were to have a baby boy. He had been such a smart kid, he could read when he was two. He had become spellbound with the piano when he was three and Marie had taught him how to pick out simple tunes on it. The piano was discarded when a well-meaning relation had bought Joey a toy guitar one Christmas. He soon grew tired of that and demanded a real guitar. Books and school were forgotten, the guitar was played day and night. Marie had loved to hear him play and with her gentle encouragement he had still managed to do well in school. But then she had got sick . . .

Mr Boland jerked awake. The clock struck five. He was glad he had awoken as he did not want to think about that nightmare period in his life. Joey had been impossible at that time and he had become even more impossible since. Marie had died and now Joe might – no, he wouldn't even think of that scenario. He willed life into his son and still there was no response.

At six a young doctor came in to check on Joe. He looked at the monitors and fiddled with things. He turned to Mr Boland and gave a brief smile. "He seems to have stabilised. I can't promise anything more but it does look good."

Pete Boland breathed a shaky sigh. Things were improving. His mind was still grovelling with any God that existed to spare Joe. He couldn't take it again. Not again.

Chapter Seventeen

It was the pain that woke him. His head was pounding and his leg and ribs were terribly sore. His right arm was numb. Slowly he tried to open his eyes. They seemed to be swollen or something. Dimly, he made out the room he was in. He wasn't at home – where the hell was he? He couldn't have drunk that much last night, surely? He had never had a hangover this bad before.

He tried again to move his arm but it wouldn't budge, there seemed to be a weight on it. With difficulty, he managed to move his head around and he saw someone lying across his arm.

"Hey – me bleedin' arm." He was surprised when his voice wouldn't work too well. It came out sounding like a whisper.

"Hey." He tried to make his voice louder this time and the man stirred and then jerked awake. With some surprise, Joey recognised his Da. The two stared at one other, Joey puzzled and his father with total wonder and relief on his face.

"Joe," he said cautiously. "Are you OK?"

"Me bleedin' arm," Joe mumbled before he blacked out again.

Mr Boland rang for the doctor, he did not stop ringing until the doctor entered the ward.

"What – what's the matter?"

"He woke up. He talked – I don't know what he said, but he's gone again," Pete Boland explained frantically.

The doctor grinned. "That's one strong kid," he said in admiration. "If he woke – he'll be fine. He's probably just weak." He proceeded to run a check on Joe and then grinning again shook Pete's hand and said, "If I were you, I'd get some sleep. He'll be fine."

Pete Boland collapsed onto the chair. He couldn't believe it. He decided to ring Chris and Dee to tell them the news. It was seven o'clock and they should be getting up. He also ran into the casualty waiting room and informed Joe's twenty tired mates that he was going to be fine. The cheering woke up the whole floor and they were told sternly to be quiet by the nurse on duty.

"Any chance we can see him?" Mick asked.

Mr Boland nodded. "I'll let you in to see him later, Mick. I don't know about everyone else."

"Don't worry 'bout us, Mr B," Stephen said cheerfully. "We'll head home now that the news is good."

They all began to get into their coats and jackets, the mood in the room suddenly transformed into a carnival-like atmosphere.

Mick was suddenly left on his own in an empty room. Ann and Cathy had made Mick promise to ring them as soon as he'd seen Joe.

Irene came in and smiled at Mick. In her hand she held a mug of tea and a plate of toast. He gratefully accepted them from her and she asked him how he was.

"Fine," he said. "Listen, sorry for goin' off the deep end at you last night. I was in bits."

"It's OK," she smiled. "I've heard worse." There

was a silence broken only by the sound of Mick eating. Then Irene said, "He's a popular guy, isn't he?"

Mick nodded and grinned. "Yeah, he's a great laugh." He stopped and said cautiously, "I know he's given you a hard time – he's told me – but he's not really like that, you'll see."

Irene stood up. "Drop the mug back into my office when you're finished," she said abruptly. "I'll give you a shout when you can go and see him."

Joey had been awake since ten o'clock. His father had gently explained everything to him and memory was slowly beginning to come back. He began to tremble violently as he looked at his bruised hands and legs. He owed a major debt to Ann and the rest of his mates for following him.

The cops had been in at ten-fifteen and he had failed to give a positive ID on his attackers. He suspected that it had been Kendell but unfortunately he couldn't prove it.

He was alone with his father when they left. They stared at each other awkwardly. His Da was the first to speak. He cleared his throat and said shakily, "I never ever meant to hurt you, Joe. I'm deeply sorry for what I said to you about musicians last night and all the other stuff we argued about –" he faltered and then continued, "Can't we just put it in the past and try and live with each other?"

Joey bit his lip and eyed his Da warily. Then nodding slowly he held out his hand. He tried to grin as he said, "I will if you will."

Pete Boland clasped his son's hand in his and the two smiled at each other for the first time in months.

Joey was moved to Irene's ward that evening. It was meant to be a surprise for Irene as the staff had been

106

told that he was her step-son to be. It did not impress her or her future step-son.

"There is a visitor for you," she said briskly, talking to him as if he were just another patient. "He's been waiting all day, so I said I'd let him have a few minutes with you."

Joey did not reply. He was not going to make it easy for her just because he and his Da had kind of patched up their differences.

"Well, I must give congrats to Kendell on his handy-work, that face is a definite improvement!" Mick announced, shocking the other six patients.

Joey laughed. "I haven't seen it yet an' I figure I don't want to."

"It'll clear up," Mick said, unable to stop grinning ridiculously at him. "Jaysus, Joe," he breathed. "You give us all one hell of a shock. Poor Ann was in bits." Then nodding he declared, "It's great to see you."

"NURSE!"

Irene came running. Mick and Joey looked at the frail old man in the next bed.

"Yes, Mr Hanley?" Irene looked questioningly at him.

"Why has that lad got a visitor at this time in the day?"

Irene explained to him as Mick and Joe grinned.

"I am trying to sleep," he grumbled. "The obscene language I have heard them use is shocking!"

Irene glared at the two lads. She walked over to Joey and whispered fiercely, "Will you try and have a bit of respect for the other patients, please!" Then turning to Mr Hanley she smiled as she said, "It's all under control now."

She stalked out as Mr Hanley looked triumphantly at them.

"Wagon!" Joey mumbled. "I dunno why they stuck me with her."

"She's all right," Mick said cautiously. "She was dead on last night. She brought us in tea at about four in the mornin'. She let us use her phone. She's OK, Joe."

"Yeah, sure!" Joey knew he was going to hate it here.

Ann arrived in at seven the next night. She gazed at Joe and grinned. "I've got good news," she announced. "Are you ready for it?"

He was delighted to see her. He laughed, his face hurting as he did so. "How are you, Joe. You're lookin' better," he slagged her.

"Shut up," she giggled. "Well, do you want to hear?"

"NURSE!"

Joey raised his eyes to heaven. Mr Hanley had been moaning all day.

"Yes?" Irene, red-faced entered.

"It's half an hour before visiting – how is it that there is yet another early visitor at that lad's bed? She is even cursing!"

Irene thought the old man was going to have a coronary.

"Joe?" She turned to him for an explanation.

Ann answered for him. "I said 'Shut up'."

Irene suppressed a smile. "It won't happen again." She placated the old man. "I told Ann she could visit Joe early, just for today. They'll be quiet."

He continued to grumble to himself but Ann and Joey ignored him.

"Well?" Joey asked.

"Can't you guess?" Ann's eyes were shining.

Joey shook his head. "Naw."

"What's the best news you could hear – right at this minute?"

"That the oul fella over there had his voice box removed?"

Ann laughed. "I see your accident hasn't made you more understanding," she slagged. Then she asked, eyebrows raised, "Do the words 'third round' mean anything to you?"

"WHAT?" Joey howled with delight. "WHEN DID YA HEAR THIS?"

Six people in the ward jumped. Mr Hanley yelled for Irene who chose to ignore him.

Ann broke up in a fit of giggling. Stammering, Joey apologised to everyone.

"When did you find out?" he whispered.

"About an hour ago. The judges rang Trev and he rang me. I decided to tell you before Trev got a chance. I never told him I was coming in early tonight."

Joey laughed. "He'll go mad."

Ann tossed her head back. "I don't care, he always gets to tell everyone all the news, so I said, feck him."

"Oh, ya girl ya!"

Domo, Trev and Mick came in at seven-thirty. Trev laughed when he heard what Ann had done. "I knew you would," he grinned at her. "That's why I told you first."

Talk then turned to the band.

When Joe's Dad and sisters entered about ten minutes later, Mick turned to them saying, "Hey, Mr B isn't it great about the band?"

Joey sucked in his breath. "Oh, oh."

"What band?"

"Us. We got into the third round of The Battle of the Bands."

"Oh, really?" He shot Joe a sharp look – what the hell was Mick talking about?

"It's great – isn't it?"

"Oh, yes indeed. Fantastic." He was out of his depth. Chris and Dee looked just as confused.

"Just as bleedin' well the finals are in October. Joe would scare the hell out of anyone lookin' at him at the moment."

Mr Boland was shocked. What a thing to say. This fella was Joe's best friend! He couldn't believe it when Joe said, "Aw, Micko, don't make me laugh, me ribs are killin' me."

Obviously his son had a weird sense of humour.

At nine, all the visitors left and there had been some amount of them. They had eaten all the fruit that someone had left on Joe's locker. Joe kept forcing them to finish it and they didn't need to be told twice. Mr Boland thought that they would never leave. They had all been raving about this Battle of the Bands thing. Joe had got more and more guilty looking as time went on.

After the last convoy had gone, Pete Boland placed both his hands on either side of Joey and hissed, "What the hell is happening in October and what on earth is Battle of the Bands?"

Joe gulped. "Well, Da, me and the lads entered a competition an' eight bands get into the finals. We are one of them." He looked at his sisters. "We'll be on the telly."

"So how come we never heard this before?" His Da was annoyed. So were Dee and Chris.

"You weren't interested, were you?" Joey felt quite defensive.

"YOU NEVER BOTHERED TO FIND OUT – DID YOU?" His father shouted.

"NURSE – NURSE – NURSE!" Mr Hanley shouted.

Joey tried to stop laughing. His Da was mortified.

110

Irene came in and had to listen to a barrage of complaint about the rowdy man at the next bed. She shot Pete a filthy look, told him crossly to keep his voice down and advanced on Joey. "You might like to give me a hard time out of this hospital, but I am warning you, I can make it twice as hard for you in here."

"It wasn't his fault –" his Da tried to say but she cut him short by marching out.

Joey's eyes were laughing and Chris and Dee tried to stop their own giggles.

Mr Boland failed to see any humour in the situation. Turning once again to his son he said, "We would have been interested, you jerk! We would have been so excited –"

"I get six free tickets – you can come. Dee an' Chris an' three others if you want – that is?" Joey despised the plea in his voice.

His father gazed at him. "I just can't figure you out," he sounded puzzled. "You spend your life trying to prove that this band is great. Then when you actually achieve something you don't tell us."

Joey bit his lip and said nothing. He had hoped that his Da would have jumped at the chance to come and see him. It didn't look as if that was going to happen.

"What date in October is it on?" his Da asked.

Joey shrugged. "Dunno, I only heard myself today."

"So do you want us to keep that day free?"

Joey shrugged. "It's up to you," he said quietly.

Mr Boland looked at Joe's blond head. "I wouldn't miss it for the world," he said. Father and son grinned at each other.

Chris sat beside him on the bed. "So, tell us about it from the beginning, baby bruv. If you're going to be a TV star, I'll have to be well informed to be able to give interviews."

Chapter Eighteen

Joey was in hospital for two weeks and he hadn't found it too bad as Irene hadn't bothered him much. She stayed pretty much out of his way.

When Mr Hanley left, he bought Irene a box of chocolates. There was a stunned silence in the ward as he told everyone that she was his favourite nurse. She had hugged him and everyone had laughed.

Joey was standing in the hall waiting for his Da to pick him up. His left leg was still in plaster and he had a crutch. The bruises on his face had mostly cleared up and his stitches had been removed. There was a bit of a scar but Joe thought it gave him a tough look as did his broken nose.

Irene was writing at her desk. She looked at him. "You got everything?" she asked briskly.

He nodded.

"Good." She put her head down and continued writing.

"Irene?" His heart was hammering.

She looked up in annoyance. "What is it?" she asked impatiently.

"Thanks," he mumbled.

She was about to make a sharp retort when something in his face stopped her. He meant it! It wasn't a smart remark, the kid meant it! Smiling, she put the pen in her mouth and looked at him thoughtfully. "It was no problem. You were a model patient."

"Yeah, well," Joey stared down at his feet.

She took a deep breath and decided that it was now or never. Steeling herself she said, "I know how you feel about me, Joe, and I can't say I wouldn't feel the same in your shoes." Joey looked at her in surprise as she went on, "I just want you to know that I love your Dad very much. I don't want to replace your Mother and frankly if I thought that Pete was trying to use me as his wife's replacement, I wouldn't touch him with a barge pole. He'll never forget your Ma either."

Joey's face took on a sulky look. "I was only thankin' you for lookin' after me. I don't want a lecture."

"Oh, for goodness' sake," Irene exclaimed impatiently. "I am only trying to explain things to you so that life can be easier for all of us. I am sick of being treated like a leper every time I meet you – it can't go on, Joe."

He said nothing. Why had he bothered?

"I've a feeling you won't let yourself like me." Irene began to walk toward him. "Please, Joe, give me a break. I've begun to like you these last two weeks – you could really make the other patients laugh. Just give me a chance. I promise I don't want to be your mother."

Joey cracked a grin. "I'm not bleedin' surprised!" They both began to laugh and then there was a silence.

"Well?" Irene asked.

Joey shrugged, torn by guilt. It was true, he did like her but he felt as if he was betraying his real mother. "I'll try," he agreed reluctantly. "I still would prefer though, if you weren't gettin' married at all." With these words he turned his back on Irene and began to walk away.

His Da took him home in the car. There was a comfortable silence betweem them during the drive. Joey thought that his Da seemed a bit edgy though, like as if he wanted to say something and then kept backing away.

When they arrived at the house, Mr Boland took Joey's case from him and placed it in the hallway. Then taking a deep breath he said, "Come on into the kitchen and we'll have a cuppa."

Joey looked around the hallway, touched the fresco wallpaper and smelled the sweet smell of home. He never thought that he would have missed it so much. In the kitchen his Da had the kettle boiled and was pouring him a cup of tea – ultra weak. His Da's tea was always terrible.

When Joey had sat down Mr Boland, placing his elbows on the table and looking intently at his son, began to speak.

"Joe, I feel I have to say this to you. I will probably never get such an ideal chance again." He attempted a smile which his son did not return.

Joey wondered what was coming.

His father took a deep breath and continued, "I'm not sorry about my views, Joe, but you're right, it is your life and I'll try not to interfere any more."

Joey's eyes widened in disbelief. He slowly turned to face his Da. "You really mean tha'?"

Mr Boland shrugged. "I have no choice. I want to keep my son, not drive him from me."

"Thanks, Da." Joey attempted a grin. "You won't regret this."

He was hurt the way his father said cuttingly, "I just hope you don't."

There was another silence. It was hard to talk to this lad who was his flesh and blood. He had something else to add to this conversation and he decided to strike while the iron was hot.

"There is one thing you have to realise, of course." Joey eyed him cautiously.

"I have admitted that you have your life and that I won't interfere in it, so I think you should repay the favour." He moved in closer to his son and said, "You stay out of telling me how to run my life. Don't dictate to me whether I can marry or not – all right!"

Joey's eyes grew hostile.

His father, undaunted, continued, "Irene and I love each other. She is not out to replace your mother. How could I forget your ma? How could I, when she gave me three great kids?"

"You're bloody selfish," Joey spat out, startling his Da. "How can you do it to me Ma? How can you replace her so easily?"

"Don't talk to me about selfish!" Mr Boland shouted, unable to stop himself. He leaned across the table saying slowly and deliberately, "You were selfish when your mother was dying. Where was the devoted son then, huh?"

Joey went pale. His eyes filled with tears. "Oh, Jesus," he moaned as he brought his hands to his face.

"Joe, Joe," Mr Boland said hastily. "I didn't mean that, I was angry, Joe, please . . ."

Joey couldn't hear him, he was back in that time

three years ago, that time he had spent so long trying to block out . . .

There was a silence in the room. Chris broke it by hurling herself at her mother and crying, "Please say it's not true, Ma. Please."

His Da had his arm around his Ma and his eyes were red.

Dee asked, "Did you go for a second opinion, Ma?" Then, her voice rising in hysteria, she said, "Surely they can operate."

Their Ma shook her head. "They said it was too risky." Her voice broke. "The tumour is too deep."

He looked at the scene as if he were someone else. That woman had a brain tumour. She had only a few months left – maybe till Christmas. Thank God he didn't have to stay here. He got up to leave.

"Joe, where are you going?" his Da asked.

"Out to a gig with Mick."

There was a shocked silence. "You are joking," his Da's voice.

He looked at them and at the woman. "No, I promised him."

She got really bad. She had nightmares and fits. She couldn't walk one day and the next she could. She had treatment that made her sick.

His Da used to go mad at him. "Why wouldn't you help your mother this morning, did you not hear her calling?" he'd yell.

"No."

He didn't like being in the house when she was there. He went out all the time. He even stayed late studying at school, he was always up in Mick's.

He sometimes heard her crying but he couldn't go

116

near her. His legs stopped him. Once, he heard her laughing in the kitchen with his sister, Chris, and he had put his hand on the door knob to join them but then he remembered and went out.

He had fought with Mick over her. Mick had said, "Joe, I never knew your Ma was sick. I'm really sorry."

"For what?"

"Huh?"

"What are you bleedin' sorry for?"

"I'm sorry for you and your family and your Ma." Mick sounded puzzled.

"We are fine, Mick."

"Joe, I don't think you are handling this too well. You never seem to be in with your family and they need you now. Are you –"

He had grabbed Mick and shoved him up against a wall. "Shut your bleedin' mouth. Don't piss me off! Don't talk to me about me family. Just shut your mouth, Mick." He had left Mick then and bunked off school for the day. He couldn't even remember where he had gone.

Mick had never mentioned the subject again. He had hung around Joe though and gone out with him everywhere and invited him back to his house to stay and stuff. They had never talked about the row.

He kept trying to avoid the woman. Eventually, his Da and his sisters stopped askin' him to help her. He was glad.

On his birthday his Da told him that his present was in the boxroom. He had gone upstairs to get it and she had been in there holding it.

"Joe," she said in a soft voice. He noticed she looked terrible.

She held out the present – "Happy Birthday."

His arms would not move to take it and her eyes filled with tears. She walked toward him and left it beside him saying, in a slow voice that wasn't hers, "Always remember, I love you Joe." She put her frail hand against his cheek and he flinched away from it.

"Always remember, I love you, Joe."

She died two weeks later. He did not go in to see the body. He carried the coffin at the funeral, dry-eyed. He had never cried over her or mentioned her since . . .

"I'm sorry, Joe," Mr Boland was in a panic.

Joey turned tortured eyes toward him and through bitter tears, Mr Boland made out the words, "I was cryin' inside Da, I was crying inside for her."

"What – for who?"

"Me Ma, I was cryin' an' it wouldn't come out. Everyone thought I didn't care. I couldn't bear it, Da. I can't bear to think what I did to her. I was cryin' inside."

With growing horror, Pete Boland realised that these were tears that should have been shed three years ago. His son had bottled this up for three years. Awkwardly he cradled Joe in his arms. Oh, it felt good to hold him close.

Joey cried for a long time as his Da, stroking his hair gently said, "Let it out, Joe. Just let it go."

Mick called up that evening. "How's it goin'?" he asked grinning. He noticed Joe's crutch in the corner of the room and decided to have a go of it. "Wow, that's hard enough to use," he remarked as he rubbed his arm. Then noticing Joey's lack of response he raised his eyebrows and asked, "What's up, Boland?"

Joey didn't know quite how to start. He decided to go straight for it. "I owe you an apology, Mick."

Mick looked puzzled. "For what?"

Joey bit his lip. "It's hard to explain. Do you remember that time when me Ma was . . . was . . . dying?"

Mick nodded slowly.

"Well," Joey said, gazing at Mick, "I'm sorry for pinnin' you up against the wall. I know you've been a bit edgy with me ever since an' I'm sorry. I don't want to get all bleedin' sentimental, but you're me best mate an' I've treated you like shit."

Mick just stared.

"Well, say somethin', you asshole. Don't feckin' leave me feelin' like a thick. I've just apologised for somethin' that happened three years ago an' as they say better late than bleedin' never." There had been a subtle change in Joe, Mick could tell. The guarded look was gone, the look that wouldn't allow people too close.

Mick grinned at him. He laughed as he said, "You and your apology can go an' piss off. I've waited for ages for you to say that an' just cause I bleedin' save your life you decide to be nice to me."

Chapter Nineteen

The day of the competition dawned. Joey was awake early. He watched the first fingers of daylight steal into his room.

Looking at his clock, he decided that it was far too early to get up. He began to think about the last two months since he had been beaten up and everything that had happened.

It had been weird! Everyone was talking to him again. His Da had been as good as his word and had not interfered in his life. He had been delighted, however, when Joe had announced that he had found himself a part-time job – working as a relief barman in The Coach House. At least now, his Da said, he was a little on his way to becoming independent. If he was disappointed in his son's choice of work, he didn't say.

Mick did get his college course and Joe had to suppress a grin when Mick announced it in his house. His Da had to plaster a smile on his face and congratulate Mick while looking daggers at his own son. Joe had pretended not to notice.

Irene and Joe had a cordial relationship. He didn't give her a hard time anymore. He even smiled at her on occasion, but he never let himself really enjoy her company. That was something he had decided on until he got his head sorted.

"Joe!" Dee's voice broke into his thoughts. "I'm leaving now, I'll see you later tonight. Good luck!"

"Yeah, good luck, baby bruv," Chris poked her head around his door also. "I can't wait to see you lot strut your stuff tonight."

"Yeah, thanks," Joey replied sleepily as he crawled out of bed. It was going to be a busy day. Trev wanted them all at the concert hall for two-thirty. He was driving them in his Da's car. They had to have a technical rehearsal at three o'clock.

Joey hastily began to pack the gear that he was wearing onstage before his Da saw it. His Da was convinced that he was going to be wearing some pair of desperate trousers that he had made Dee buy for him. Joe hadn't told him that the band were all wearing jeans. He didn't think his Da would understand.

Finished packing, he went downstairs to grab some breakfast. His Da was in the kitchen. "Tea?" he asked and Joey nodded.

"Today's the day – huh?"

Joey nodded.

"Nervous?"

"Naw, not so far. Trev's bad enough for the rest of us though." He began to pour some flakes into a bowl.

"How's the little girl doing?" His Da always referred to Ann as "the little girl". He seemed to have taken a fancy to her ever since she had spied the fellas trying to jump Joey.

"Great," Joey said, his mouth stuffed. "Great voice. We're fourth on tonight – the last band before the interval."

Mr Boland went over to the worktop and lifted a

navy pair of trousers down. He handed them to Joey saying, "Dee ironed them for you this morning. Don't forget to pack them."

"Thanks," he said taking them from his father and trying to not to smile.

"Irene bought a new suit for tonight," Mr Boland said. "You'd think she was the one going to be on the telly."

"Her last spend before the big day, huh?"

Mr Boland's heart leaped. He wanted to hug the breath out of his son. This was the first time he had mentioned the wedding.

"Yeah, she's making the most of her freedom. Next year she'll be a married woman."

Joey idly stirred his tea. "When next year?" he asked in a quiet voice, his smile gone.

"July," Mr Boland said gently.

There was a silence. Mr Boland cleared his throat and said hesitantly, "Seeing as we are on the subject, Joe, Irene and I were wondering if you . . . if you would be my best man?"

"Huh?"

"You heard." Pete Boland gazed at Joey's bent head, wishing he could see the expression on his face. He felt relieved that he had eventually asked Joe. It was a weight off his mind. Irene had been pestering him about it for ages.

"Your best man?" Joey looked solemnly at his Da.

"You don't have to decide at once, Joe. If you refuse, we'll understand. Let me know when you make up your mind."

"Sure. Sure Da."

His father picked up his coat from the chair saying, "Well, I'm off. Good luck tonight, Joe. We'll see you afterwards."

With that he was gone and Joey was left alone in the house, his head swimming – his Da's best man! What the hell was he going to do?

Ann was in a state when Mick and Joey arrived at her door. "We're late," she wailed at them.

"Blame him!" Mick pointed crossly at Joe who beamed at Ann saying, "He'd drive you bleedin' mad. He's like an ould one going on."

Ann tried her best not to smile in return. Joe thought that once he grinned he could get away with anything. "Trev'll have a fit," she announced. "He was bad enough at rehearsal last night."

"Good point!" Mick glared at Joey who was unruffled.

"Tell him me leg was sore and I had to limp along."

Ann gave a shout of laughter as she said, "Oh, Joe that's awful. Mocking is catching."

She pulled down the hood of her jacket. "Got my hair done, do you's like it?"

Mick couldn't believe the change a haircut could make. She had it done in a short layered bob and it really suited her.

"It's nice, Ann," Joey said innocently. "Did you do it yourself?"

Ann hit him for saying that and turning to Mick, Joey said, "You're right Mick, she does do body buildin'."

Mick watched in amusement as the two began to trade merry insults. "I might as well not be here," he thought to himself, "For all the notice they're takin' of me."

"A battle royal by eight of Ireland's most promising bands is forecast for tonight," Domo read to them from the *Irish Independent* as they sped through Ranelagh on their way to the Point Depot. "The eight were chosen from fifteen hundred original entries. A preview of the eight is on page eight."

Domo pulled the paper apart in his eagerness to find page eight.

"Here we are," he said. "Livewire: A five member band with a female vocalist."

"That's it?" Mick was disappointed.

"Yeah," Domo replied. "Well, what else can they say? We're not exactly well known."

"Tell us who the other bands are," Trev instructed from the front seat.

"Eh – The Mavericks, High Treason, Pieces of Eight, Shuttleforce, Manchua, The Glow Worms and Washington DC."

"Washington DC," Joey groaned. "I've bleedin' heard of them. The're great. They do a regular spot in The Garda Club.

"Yeah, I know them too," Domo announced. "They've got a great looking guitarist."

"Trust you," Trev said in disgust. "We are talkin' about what kind of music they play and all you can worry about is their lead guitarist."

"Bass."

"What?"

"She's their bass guitarist, Trev."

"Any one else know the other bands?" Trev chose to ignore Domo. He was annoying him like mad today.

"So these are our dressing rooms . . ." Ann looked around. She was glad that at least there was a small connecting room for her to change in; she didn't want to change in front of four fellas.

Trev opened a wardrobe. "We can hang our gear in here, lads. They've provided hangers an' all."

There was a knock on the door and a woman carrying a clipboard entered. "Livewire?"

They nodded. She smiled at them saying, "I'm just going to give you a run-down on what to do today. Firstly, your tech is scheduled from three o'clock to four. After that you can do what you like. We need you all back here by seven for make-up. As you are the fourth band on, you can expect to take the stage at around nine-fifteen. Try not to go over fifteen minutes on the songs. By the way, there is a television over there." She pointed to a portable sitting on a small table. "You can plug it in and watch the rest of the bands." Then, smiling at each of them, she said, "The best of luck to you all!"

There was a silence when she left. Ann was positive she could feel her breakfast coming up.

The tech had been completed, they had eaten in Supermacs and now, at seven-thirty, the atmosphere was electric. Ann said she felt sick and Domo calmly informed her that as she had eaten nothing that afternoon, nothing would come up.

"Christ, Dom, will you stop!" Trev snapped.

"Steady on, Trev," Mick said. "He's only messin'."

"Pity he isn't bleedin' nervous," Trev said sulkily. "I know I am at the way he plays."

Domo gave a loud laugh at that. "There is no point in both of us worryin' about it, is there, Trev?"

At that Trev grinned. He apologised to Domo, saying, "You know what I'm like before things like this."

"Cool, calm an' collected," Joey slagged.

"Yeah, like yerself," Trev retorted, pulling on his denim shirt.

Ann yelled from her room, "Is it safe to come in now? I'm ready."

"If you want the thrill of a lifetime, come out now," Joey yelled.

"Why?" Ann sounded suspicious.

"Don't mind him, Ann," Mick said. "He's only jokin'."

She emerged from the toilet in a peach body top, denim shirt and ripped denim jeans.

"You look well," Trev said approvingly. "Denims suit you."

"All the one colour suits you," Joey laughed.

The make-up artist arrived in and swiftly applied their make-up. "It's for the lights," she exclaimed to the four dismayed lads. "If I don't put it on you'll look too pale."

There was a silence when she left. Ann felt pale through all the make-up. Joey went off into a corner and began to strum on his guitar, tightening up his strings.

Mick broke the quiet by saying, "Well, lads, all I can say is that yez look gorgeous."

"I think I look lovely," Joey replied, patting his hair, and Trev began to sing, "If My Friends Could See Me Now".

Chapter Twenty

"Tickets," the doorman said. Mr Boland produced his six tickets. "Thank you, sir, if you all will follow me."

Pete Boland, Irene, Chris and boyfriend, Gerry, Dee and her boyfriend Tom, were led to their seats. It was seven-thirty and the place was filling up. They saw Mick's mother about two seats in front and she came up to talk to them. About ten minutes later, there was an announcement: "Ladies and gentlemen, will you please take your seats. Mr Fanning will be on the stage shortly."

"Who the hell is that?" Pete Boland grumbled.

"Dave Fanning, Da. He discovered U2. He knows more about music than anybody." Chris was shocked at her Da's ignorance.

"Does he, indeed?" Pete Boland was not impressed. He had thought someone like Gay Byrne would be the MC.

Chris grinned at Irene who was trying not to laugh.

People began to return to their seats and about five minutes later, Dave Fanning appeared.

"Hiya folks!" he said in his flat Dublin accent. He waited for the clapping to cease before leaning in toward the microphone. "We will be on air in about ten minutes. I just want to say that as the programme is live, please give each of our bands a big round of applause after they finish their performance. They have all done great to get here."

"YAHOO!" yelled someone and there was a moment's laughter.

"Secondly, I don't want anyone to leave their seats during the performance. You might distract the band on stage. There will be ad breaks at eight-fifty and nine-thirty so's you can leave your seats then. Thanks for your co-operation and see you at five past eight." He walked off stage to the sound of cheering.

"Dreadful voice," Pete Boland muttered, still unimpressed.

Back in the dressing-room nerves were fraying – especially Domo's. He had been the calmest of the lot up to this moment, but hearing the muffled voice of Fanning and the applause had totally unnerved him.

"How many does this place hold?" he asked.

The others shrugged, too sick to speak.

They had agreed to watch the very start of the Battle on the television, but they were not going to watch any of the bands until they had been on stage themselves.

Trev went over and switched on Network 2. They held their breath as the announcer said, "And now we go live to The Point for the competition that everyone is talking about – the new comer band of the year award!"

Rapturous applause. Fanning grinned as he stood on a podium to the left of the stage. Royal blue curtains behind him. Three quarters of the nation tuned in. Eyes of the audience glued to the stage. Big Neilson ratings for RTE.

Dave Fanning welcomed everyone to the concert hall. He promised a great night and then introduced the judges. "The prize is being sponsored by Murphy's Meats who, as we all know, like to encourage

128

youngsters in the arts and what better way to spend their money." There was stamping and cheering.

"The chairman of the board is Mr Colm Murphy of Murphy's Meats."

There was cheering as Colm stood up and acknowledged the applause.

The other judges were Mary Black, Paul McGuinness, Pat Egan who was a promotions manager and Bono from U2. His presence alone counted for the major interest in the contest.

"Now, down to business," Dave Fanning consulted his notes as the clapping died down. "The first band is Washington DC and their name is no accident . . ."

Ann had vomited. "It's OK," she smiled wanly around at the four anxious faces. "I feel better now. It's just nerves – honest."

Joey pulled up a chair and made her sit down. "I'll do the singin' if you want," he joked.

"We wouldn't have much of a hope then," she smiled. She gazed at her pale face in the mirror and exclaimed, "Oh, God, I look awful! Has anyone got a comb?" She began to run her hands through her hair.

"You look great," Joey said. "Leave your hair alone, it's beautiful."

Ann looked up at him and nodding he said, "Honest it is," before turning abruptly away from her.

There was a rap on the door and a man entered. "Livewire?"

They nodded.

"Get your gear and follow me."

Joey and Trev picked up their guitars. Domo's drums and Mick's keyboard were backstage and stage hands would move them on when the time came. Trev had his hand on Ann's shoulder and giving it a reassuring squeeze, he said, "You'll be great, Ann. Don't worry." She managed a watery smile in return.

Shuttleforce were just coming off stage. They whispered "Good luck" as they passed which Ann thought was really nice. Very quietly, the backstage men began assembling their equipment.

"Here they are now!" Dee dug her nails into Tom's arm in nervous excitement.

"And now, our last band before the interval. They are relative newcomers to the scene. They only acquired their lead singer earlier this year –"

Pete Boland gulped. "Oh, God, Irene, what if he drops his guitar or they forget the songs or –"

"Will you shush," Irene said sternly. "Think of how they're feeling."

The curtain swished back and the stage was in complete darkness . . .

Ann was afraid her voice wouldn't come. But once Mick began to play the first gentle bars of "Do You Remember?" she began to relax slightly. She loved this song the best of the three. It was sheer poetry. Backed by Mick and Joey she began to sing softly, her voice swelling and filling the hall.

"Sometimes when I'm sad and need a place to hide,
Sometimes when I'm lonely an' life's a bumpy ride,
I close my eyes an' think of you
an' everythin' that's fresh an' new
Comes rushin' to my mind.
Together Mick and Ann sang:
"Do you remember what you said to me?
Do you remember what you said that day?
Do you remember what you said to me?
Before you went away – I love you, I love you,

I love you forever – before you went away.
Before you went away.
Ann continued, growing in confidence:
"Sometimes in the night time,
When I'm feelin' really low,
I hear your voice on the breeze,
Melodious and slow, saying:
"Do you see the stars as they light the earth so bright,
Don't you know it's just my way of sayin' to you goodnight.
The poetry of the song lulled the audience.
" . . . You made this world a crazy poem.
An' me its humble scribe.
But it can never compare to you
No matter how it tries . . .

The song ended, but they had worked a way of going from one song to the other without stopping. Ann began to enjoy herself and the lads heaved a sigh of relief – they had really been freaked when she had got sick. They started into the second song . . .

"Excellent song," Irene's voice was frank with admiration, "Who wrote it?"

"Mick did, I think," Mr Boland whispered. "Joe says Mick writes all their stuff." He was half angry and half proud. He had nearly died when he had seen the get-up of them. To think Joe should appear on national telly in a pair of torn denims. Once the music had started, he had swelled with pride. Joe was good – they were all good. He sat there beaming and Dee and Irene had exchanged smiles. Tom, Dee's boyfriend, was enjoying himself. The first song was nice and the number they were doing now wasn't bad either. He wondered what the third song was like. Judging by the other bands, usually the best was kept for last.

The lights dimmed and the music of the second song

dulled into stillness. Silence for a second. Domo gulped, he hoped that he could get the feckin' drum beat right.

Ann's voice broke the stillness. "In Xanadu did Kubla Khan . . . down to a sunless sea."

Domo began to play, a low threatening beat. He gave a sigh of relief, he had come in at the right place.

Domo's drums got louder as Ann continued to sing. Joey's guitar came in then and the drums and Ann's voice faded out.

A spotlight was focused on him and he began to portray the battle on his guitar. His fingers were like lightning and like his idol, Mark Knoffler, he made the guitar talk. Eventually, that too dulled into stillness and Ann's voice took over once again.

"Feckin' brilliant!" Gerry declared as he alone gave them a standing ovation. Chris dragged him down, unable to stop giggling as people glared.

Tom said, "Didn't mind them as much as I thought I would," which made Dee smile. She was on a high. She wished she could see them all over again, yet she was relieved that they had finished.

Mick's parents were passing by. "Great, weren't they?" Mick's father said proudly.

"Yes, very good." Pete Boland was beaming. Joe had been brilliant on the guitar, it was like looking at Marie all over again. She had had the same fire when she played the piano and now her talent burned in Joe. He was brilliant, absolutely brilliant!

Tears pricked his eyes and Irene found his hand and squeezed it.

"Coming for a drink?" Mick's mother asked and they all declared that they needed one.

Trev picked Ann up and swung her around. She began

to thump him on the shoulders laughing and saying, "Oh, Trev, you'll make me sick – please don't, Trev."

"You were great!" he whooped. "Wasn't she, lads – wasn't she great?"

"We were all great," Ann declared as he put her down. She laughed over at Domo. "You even got the drum beat right."

"I know, I know."

"I heard someone clapping when Joe finished his guitar solo," Mick said.

"I think we got a louder round of applause than any of the other bands," Joey declared.

"Yeah, well when you are on the stage, the applause usually sounds louder than if you are backstage!" Ann giggled.

Joey nudged her, pushing her off her seat. "I didn't mean it like that, you idiot," he said affectionately.

She thumped him. "Call me an idiot – would you?" Laughing he dodged out of her way.

"Can you two not leave each other alone," Trev slagged as Joey caught Ann by the back of the neck and held it till she begged for mercy. "Joe, let go of that girl this instant."

"With pleasure." He looked into her laughing face and his heart flip flopped. She had turned away from him and was now busy analysing the performance with Trev but he found that he couldn't take his eyes off her. He had felt like that for ages now and he wondered if she felt the same?

"It's nearly time for the second half," Mick announced, some minutes later. "Will I switch on the telly?"

The last band. Dave Fanning introduced Manchua. They were a soul band all dressed in black and white. Their music was the kind you would hear in a sleazy bar but was saved from being sleazy by their excellent lead

133

singer. He had the audience in the palm of his hand for every number. Livewire were shocked. Manchua were excellent! The standard was high, but these guys were great, or rather the singer was great.

When they had finished there was a glum silence in the dressing-room. "We'll just have to see what the judges like," was Trev's verdict.

Out in the auditorium, there was a lot of speculation going on. Gerry had declared Joe's band the winners but Chris wasn't so sure. "As far as I'm concerned there are three bands in it – the first guys, the last lot and Joe's band."

"It'll be a terrible anti-climax if they don't win," Irene said. Pete nodded. "It's a close call. The last band were great."

"I liked Shuttleforce," Dee announced. "Their violin player was great." She looked up as Tom came back with drinks for them all.

Handing them along the line he said, "The crowd in the bar think it's between Joe's band and the last lot."

"Are you serious?" Chris squealed. "Oh, God, imagine if Joe's band won! I'd be the sister of a pop star!"

The others all laughed and Gerry said, "You'd be known as the model, sister of Joe Boland."

Chris grimaced. "Ugh – I don't think I'd like that."

"Ladies and gentlemen, will you all return to your seats please. We will be on the air in approximately five minutes."

"Oh, hell." Chris felt sick. She reached for Gerry's arm and squeezed it.

Mick's mother and Cathy turned round to them and gave the thumbs up sign, which caused Dee to laugh.

The hall was filled with music. The words Band of the Year filled the television screens across the nation. Dave Fanning was spotlighted against the blue curtains.

He had changed into a formal suit. "Ladies and Gentlemen," he began, "I am pleased to announce that the judges have made their decision. Here to tell us the result is the chairman of the board, Mr Colm Murphy!"

Applause and then a dead silence as Colm began to speak. He began by saying, "OK, folks, I'm sorry to tell you that before I announce the winner, I am obliged to make one of those 'thank-you' speeches that everyone hates. Please bear with me."

Trev groaned. "I can't bear this any more. I dunno if I want to know the result. At least I've got hope now. If we lose, I'll crack up."

Joey for once agreed with him. "At least we put up a good show," he tried to console the others.

"I couldn't bleedin' care about tha'," Mick said. "If we lose I'll still be devastated."

"And now to our decision," Colm said as everywhere people waited with bated breath. "Needless to say, it was a difficult choice. We marked under various categories: material, musicianship, entertainment value and vocalists. One band scored higher than all the others in all categories. I know that eight bands are watching eagerly and that seven of them will go away disappointed. They must not be, all of the bands here tonight have the potential to go places." There was applause at this point. Colm waited until it had died down before he continued, "We have only one prize, however. The winning band will receive all the money plus the recording contract because, as you know, Murphy's Meats only support the best." More applause. "So without torturing you any further, I am pleased to announce that the band of the year award, together with a recording contract and three thousand pounds goes to none other than Livewire!"

Gerry and Chris went mad. They screamed and hugged each other.

Irene hugged Pete. Dee began to scream the house down as Tom looked on and laughed.

Mick's parents stomped like teenagers and Cathy burst into tears.

Newspaper cameras popped and flashed all over the hall as Livewire walked out on stage.

Ann was first, followed by Joey and Mick. Trev and Domo brought up the rear. They were estatic. They shook hands with Colm Murphy, who presented them with their prize. Dave Fanning went over to congratulate them. Joe was made up when he said, "I had a bet on you lads."

Dave handed Ann the microphone. There was a silence. Ann stood shyly on a stage which, just a few short hours ago, she had dominated.

Ann coughed, looked at the others and began, "All I can really do is thank the judges for selecting us and compliment them on their excellent taste!" There was laughter and she continued, "I do, however, have one special person to thank and I know the other lads in the band will agree with me on this. We couldn't have done what we did if it wasn't for the great music and lyrics. I just want to thank Joe, our lead guitarist, for writing such great stuff."

Joey grinned at her as she pointed him out. He wanted this moment to last forever.

Mr Boland was in shock. Joe had written those songs! He could have sworn . . .

The audience was shouting for an encore. Their instruments had been set up and were waiting to be played. As the credits rolled, Livewire played under the dazzling TV lights. The crowd roared their approval and the five of them realised that life would never be the same again.

Chapter Twenty-One

The reporters and TV interviewers left them alone at last.

Breathing a sigh of relief, they began to pack their gear and change into new clothes for the disco that was being held by 2FM, in the RDS. Their families would be out there when they arrived.

"Did you hear we are being driven to the disco in a limo!" Domo was awestruck.

"No less than we deserve," Joey joked. "We are TV personalities after all."

They all plastered him with their smelly socks.

Ann excused herself and went to change.

The lads were ready long before Ann was and Joey said that he would wait for her.

"Up ya boyo!" Mick jabbed him and Joey threw him a filthy look.

"Yeah, go for it Joe," Trev hissed as he passed.

"I haven't the faintest bleedin' idea what yez are on about," Joey remarked, trying to sound puzzled. He slammed the door after them, then sitting on a chair, feet up on a counter top, he waited for Ann to emerge.

"Hi, I'm ready," she startled him.

Joey looked at her. She was wearing a black dress and looked really well. She had even parted with the

Docs in favour of black shoes. "You're lookin' great," Joey remarked, trying to sound casual.

"You're not looking too bad yourself." Ann went over toward the door and opening it she asked, "Coming?"

Joey jumped up from his seat and began to follow her outside to the car. He didn't know how to start. He ended up by saying, "Do you still think I'm sexy?"

Ann looked up at him, puzzled. She was unable to recall the finer details of that famous night. "I beg your pardon?"

Joey gave a slow smile and changed tack, "Will you keep the slow dances free for me tonight?"

Ann turned round and surveyed him. "Well, Joe," she said. "I might be able to fit you in somewhere. But you know us famous people, there'll be a queue after me." She laughed, tossing her hair back.

Shit, he thought. Why the hell do I always joke about things. Now she's not takin' me seriously.

"Naw, I really mean it," Joey said aloud.

Again she laughed. "The last time you slow danced with me didn't have a very pleasant aftermath."

He grinned. "I promise not to get beaten up this time. Will you dance with me, Ann?"

"OK," she said, a slight bit impatiently. "Where's the punchline? What's the joke? You want to do me a favour cause no one else will? Come on Joe – punchline please?"

"Holy Mother of God, the girl couldn't get a hint!" Joey thought in despair.

"Punchline," he said staring around him. Then looking straight at her he said, "The punchline is that

138

I am crazy about you. I don't want any other bloke to dance with you. I want you all to myself."

Ann's heart was pounding – could he really mean it? God knows, she had fancied him for a while now. Still, she felt it might be a joke and she was not making a fool of herself for any fella.

"Tell you what," she said. "If you mean it, the first slow song that comes on tonight, you ask me to dance. I'll know you mean what you say then." With that she turned away from him, made her way toward the limo and climbed inside.

The car pulled up outside the RDS and the five emerged from it. There was a red carpet laid out for them and when they arrived inside, everyone was clapping and cheering. Ann declared that she felt really famous.

Mick pulled at Joe's arm. "Did you ask Ann out?" he enquired. "We all had a bet on it in the car."

Joe glared at him. "Thanks. I don't know why you thought I was goin' to do that."

"She said 'no' so!" Mick was trying not to laugh.

"She did not!"

"So you did ask her!"

Joey chose to ignore him. He was feeling decidedly put out. He still didn't know whether Ann would go out with him and he wouldn't be able to bear her being with anyone else. Why the hell had it taken him so long to realise that she was for him? Why the hell had he waited for so long? Joe Boland, Super Stud – what a bleedin' laugh.

As they arrived into the disco, they were swamped by their parents and families. Mick's mother hugged both Joe and Mick, tears pouring down her face.

"Well done, both of you!" she exclaimed.

Joe then found himself face to face with his Da. There was a silence between them. Mr Boland held out his hand and his voice deepened with emotion as he said, "You were brilliant, Joe – really brilliant." Joey took his hand and his Da pulled him into an embrace. "I am so proud of you, son. I am so proud of you!"

Joe closed his eyes. The words he'd waited so long to hear. His Da was proud of him! His Da was proud of him! Without thinking, he said, "Well, it's just as well you said that 'cause every groom should be proud of his best man."

His Da hugged him tighter and Irene mouthed, "Thank you" to him as she smiled at them both.

Chris and Dee lunged themselves at him then, Chris yelling at the top of her voice, "YOU'RE FAMOUS!" People turned round to stare and then laughed.

It was while Joey was talking to Gerry that he heard the first faint strains of "Love is All Around". He excused himself saying, "Sorry, Ger but I promised to do something."

He searched for Ann in the crowd and found her staring at him. He smiled and indicated the dance floor, mouthing out, "Like to dance?"

The smile she gave him made his knees go weak. It lit up her whole face and she looked beautiful.